A woman in a white flowing dress caught Cash's attention. She rushed along the side of the church. Abruptly she stopped and bent over some shrubs. What in the world was the bride doing? Looking for something?

This was certainly the most entertainment he'd had in the past half hour. He shook his head and smiled at the strange behavior. When she started running down the walk toward his vehicle he tipped his hat upward to get a better view.

The bride spun around. Her fearful gaze met his. Her pale face made her intense green eyes stand out bright with fear. Alarm tightened his chest. Was there more going on here than a change of mind?

She glanced over the hood of his truck. He followed her line of vision, spotting a group of photographers rounding the corner of the church. In the next second she'd opened his passenger door and vaulted inside.

What in the world was she doing? Planning to steal his truck?

He swung open the driver's door and climbed in.

"What are you doing in here?"

The fluffy material of her dress hit him in the face as she turned in the seat and slammed her door shut.

"Drive. Fast."

Dear Reader,

Have you ever made plans for your future? Did you think you had it all figured out? I know I did once upon a time…long, long ago. But what happens when those plans go awry?

Well, Meghan is about to find out. She has every aspect of her life planned out, down to the finest detail. So when her life spins out of control it's at the absolute worst possible time. All dolled up in her gorgeous wedding gown, she walks down the aisle only to watch her magical moment morph into a nightmare right before her eyes.

Cash wants nothing more than a quiet life, but things spring into a flurry of action when he ends up the driver of Meghan's getaway vehicle.

I hope you'll tighten your seat belt and hang on for a bumpy ride as Meghan and Cash figure out that sometimes the best things happen when you least expect them.

Happy reading!

Jennifer

JENNIFER FAYE

Rancher to the Rescue

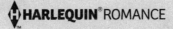

ISBN-13: 978-0-373-74251-6

RANCHER TO THE RESCUE

First North American Publication 2013

Printed in U.S.A.

www.Harlequin.com

In another life, **Jennifer Faye** was a statistician. She still has a love for numbers, formulas and spreadsheets, but when she was presented with the opportunity to follow her lifelong passion and spend her days writing and pursuing her dream of becoming a Harlequin author, she couldn't pass it up. These days, when she's not writing, Jennifer enjoys reading, fine needlework, quilting, tweeting and cheering on the Pittsburgh Penguins. She lives in Pennsylvania with her amazingly patient husband, two remarkably talented daughters and their two very spoiled fur babies, otherwise known as cats—but *shh*…don't tell them they're not human!

Jennifer loves to hear from readers—you can contact her via her website, www.JenniferFaye.com.

This is Jennifer Faye's first fabulous book for Harlequin!

To my real-life hero, Eric, who is the most positive, encouraging person I've ever known. Thanks for cheering me on to reach for the stars. You're my rock.

And to Bliss and Ashley—you both amaze and impress me every day. Thank you for filling my life with so much sunshine.

I'd also like to send a big thanks to my wonderful editor, Carly Byrne, for believing in my abilities and showing me the way to make my first book a reality.

CHAPTER ONE

Why do people insist on pledging themselves to each other? Love was fleeting at best—if it existed at all.

Cash Sullivan crossed his arms as he lounged back against the front fender of his silver pickup. He pulled his tan Stetson low, blocking out the brilliant New Mexico sun. From the no-parking zone he glanced at the adobe-style church, where all of the guests were gathered, but he refused to budge.

His grandmother had insisted he bring her, but there was no way he'd sit by and listen to a bunch of empty promises. Besides, he'd met the groom a few times over the years and found the guy to be nothing more than a bunch of hot air. Cash would rather spend his time wrestling the most contrary steer than have to make small talk with that blowhard.

He loosened his bolo tie and unbuttoned the collar of his white button-up shirt. Gram had insisted he dress up to escort her in and out of the church—even if he wasn't planning to stay.

What he wouldn't give to be back at the ranch in his old, comfy jeans, instead of these new black ones that were as stiff as a fence rail. Heck, even mucking out stalls sounded like a luxury compared to standing here with nothing to do.

A woman in a white flowing dress caught his attention. She was rushing along the side of the church. Abruptly she stopped and bent over some shrubs. What in the world was the bride doing? Looking for something?

This was certainly the most entertainment he'd had in the past half hour. He shook his head and smiled at the strange behavior. When she started running down the walk toward his vehicle, he tipped his hat upward to get a better view.

A mass of unruly red curls was piled atop her head while yards of white material fluttered behind her like the tail of a kite. Her face was heart-shaped, with lush lips. Not bad. Not bad at all.

Her breasts threatened to spill out of the dress, which hugged her waist and flared out over her full hips. She was no skinny-minny, but the curves looked good on her. Real good.

He let out a low whistle. She sure was a

looker. How in the world had boring Harold bagged her?

He couldn't tear his gaze from her as she stopped right next to his pickup and tried to open the tan SUV in the neighboring parking spot. Unable to gain access, she smacked her hand on the window. Obviously this lady had a case of cold feet—as in *ice cold*—and hadn't planned an escape route. At least she'd come to her senses before making the worst decision of her life.

The bride spun around. Her fearful gaze met his. Her pale face made her intense green eyes stand out bright with fear. Alarm tightened his chest. Was there more going on here than a change of mind?

She glanced over the hood of his truck. He followed her line of vision, spotting a group of photographers rounding the corner of the church. In the next second she'd opened his passenger door and vaulted inside.

What in the world was she doing? Planning to steal his truck? He swung open the driver's side door and climbed in.

"What are you doing in here?"

The fluffy material of her veil hit him in the face as she turned in the seat and slammed the door shut. "Drive. Fast."

He smashed down the material from her veil,

not caring if he wrinkled it. He'd never laid eyes on this woman before today, and he wasn't about to drive her anywhere until he got some answers. "Why?"

"I don't have time to explain. Unless you want to be front and center in tomorrow's paper, you'll drive."

His gaze swung around to the photographers. They hadn't noticed her yet, but that didn't ease his discomfort. "You didn't kill anyone, did you?"

"Of course not." She sighed. "Do you honestly think I'd be in this getup if I was going to murder someone?"

"I'm not into any Bonnie and Clyde scenario."

"That's good to know. Now that we have that straightened out, can you put the pedal to the metal and get us out of here before they find me?"

He grabbed the bride's arm and yanked her down out of sight, just before the group of reporters turned their curious gazes to his pickup. Luckily his truck sat high up off the ground, so no one could see much unless they were standing right next to it.

"What are you doing?" she protested, struggling.

"Those reporters don't know you're in here, and I don't want to be named in your tabloid drama. Stay down and don't get up until I tell you to."

His jaw tensed as he stuffed the white fluff beneath the dash. He was caught up in this mess whether he wanted to be or not.

Her struggles ceased. He fired up the truck and threw it in Reverse. Mustering some restraint, he eased down on the accelerator. Damn. He didn't want to be the driver for this bride's getaway, but what choice did he have?

He knew all about reporters—they were like a pack of starving wolves, just waiting for a juicy story. For their purposes he'd be "the other man." Scandals always made good sales—it didn't matter if you were an innocent bystander or not. In the court of public opinion, when your face hit the front page you were crucified. He should know.

Cash pulled his cowboy hat low, hoping no one would recognize him. He didn't want to draw the attention of the reporters who were searching behind rocks, shrubs and cars. There would be no quick getaway. Slow and steady.

When the bride once again attempted to sit up, he placed his hand on the back of her head.

"Hey, you!" a young reporter, standing a few yards away, shouted through the open window.

Cash's chest tightened as he pulled to a stop. "Yeah?"

"Did you see which way the bride ran?"

"She ran around back. Think there was a car waiting for her."

The reporter waved and took off. Cash eased off the brake and rolled toward the exit. He hadn't had a rush of adrenaline like this since his last showdown with a determined steer.

"What'd you say that for? You're making things worse," the bride protested, starting to sit up.

He pressed the side of her face back down. "Stay down or I'll dump you in this parking lot and let those hungry reporters have you."

"You wouldn't."

"Try me." He was in no mood to play around with some woman who didn't know what she wanted.

Now he needed to get rid of this bundle of frills so his life could return to its peaceful routine.

Before he could ask where she wanted to be dropped off she started to wiggle, bumping the steering wheel.

"Watch it." He steadied the wheel with both hands. "What are you doing down there?"

"Trying to get comfortable, but I think it's impossible. Are we away from the church yet?"

"Just approaching the parking lot exit, but don't get any ideas of sitting up until we're out of town. I'm not about to have people tracking me down and bothering me with a bunch of questions I can't answer."

"Thanks for being so sympathetic," she muttered.

He slowed down at the exit, checking for traffic before merging. "Hey, I didn't ask you to hijack my truck."

"I didn't have any other choice."

"Get cold feet?"

"No...yes. It's complicated." She squirmed some more. "I don't feel so good. Can I sit up yet?"

"No."

The rush of air through the open windows picked up the spicy, citrusy scent of the colorful bouquet she was still clutching. A part of him felt bad for her. He'd heard about how women got excited about their wedding day and, though he personally couldn't relate, he knew what it was to have a special moment ruined, like getting penalized after a winning rodeo ride.

He checked the rearview mirror. No one had followed him out of the parking lot. He let out a deep breath. So far, so good.

He tightened his fingers around the steering wheel, resisting the urge to run a soothing hand over her back. "Where am I taking you?"

"I…I don't know. I can't go back to my apartment. They'll be sure to find me."

"You're on the run?" He should have figured this was more than just a case of cold feet. "And what was up with the reporters?"

"My boss thought the wedding would be a good source of free publicity for my television show."

"You certainly will get publicity. *Runaway Bride Disappears Without a Trace*."

She groaned. Her hand pressed against his leg. The heat of her touch radiated through the denim. A lot of time had passed since a woman had touched him—back before his accident.

He cleared his throat. "I suppose at this point we should introduce ourselves. I'm Cash Sullivan."

He waited, wondering if there would be a moment of recognition. After all, he hadn't retired from the rodeo circuit all that long ago.

"Meghan Finnegan." When he didn't say anything, she continued, "I'm the Jiffy Cook on TV, and the reason those men are armed with cameras is to see this hometown girl marry a millionaire."

Nothing in her voice or mannerisms gave the slightest hint that she'd recognized his name. Cash assured himself it was for the best. His name wasn't always associated with the prestige of his rodeo wins—sometimes it was connected with things he'd rather forget. Still, he couldn't ignore the deflating prick of disappointment.

"I don't watch television," he said, gruffer than intended. "Okay, we're out of Lomas and this road doesn't have much traffic."

When she didn't say anything, he glanced over. Her complexion had gone ghostly pale, making her pink glossy lips stand out. "You feeling okay?"

"No." Her hand pressed to her stomach. "Pull over. Now."

He threw on his right-turn signal and pulled to a stop in a barren stretch of desert. Meg barreled out of the vehicle, leaving the door ajar. She rushed over to a large rock and hunched over. So this was what she'd been doing when she ran out of the church. Must be a huge case of nerves.

He grabbed some napkins from his glove compartment and a bottle of unopened water. It was tepid, but it'd be better than nothing. He exited the truck and followed her. He wasn't good with women—especially not ones who were upset and sick.

"Um…I can hold this for you." He reached for the lengthy veil.

He didn't know if he should try talking to her to calm her down or attempt to rub her back. He didn't want to make things worse. Unsure what to do, he stood there quietly until her stomach settled. Then he handed over the meager supplies.

"You okay now?" he asked, just before his cell phone buzzed.

His grandmother. How could he have forgotten about her? This bride had a way of messing with his mind to the point of forgetting his priorities.

He flipped open his phone, but before he could utter a word Gram said, "Where are you? Everyone's leaving."

"I went for a little ride. I'll be there in a few minutes."

"Hurry. You won't believe what happened. I'll tell you when you get here."

He hated the thought of going back and facing those reporters. Hopefully there'd be too much confusion with the missing bride and the exiting guests that they wouldn't remember he'd been the only one around when Meg had disappeared.

He cast a concerned look at his pale stowaway. "We have to go back."

Fear flashed in her eyes and she started shaking her head. "No. I can't. I won't."

"Why? Because you changed your mind about the wedding? I'm sure people will understand."

She shook her head. "No, they won't."

He didn't have time to make her see reason. "I have to go back to the church. My grandmother is waiting. I can't abandon her."

Meg's brow creased as she worried her bottom lip. "Then I'll wait here."

"What?" She couldn't be thinking clearly. "I can't leave you here. You're not well."

"I won't go back there. I can't face all of those people…especially my mother. And when the press spots us together they'll have a field day."

"You can hide on the floor again."

She shook her head. "We were lucky to get away with that once. With all of the guests leaving, the chances of me staying hidden are slim to none."

She had a good point, but it still didn't sit right with him. "Leaving you here in the middle of nowhere, in this heat, isn't a good idea."

"This isn't the middle of nowhere. I'm within walking distance of town. I'll be fine. Just go. Your grandmother is waiting. There's just one thing."

"What's that?"

"Leave me your cell phone."

He supposed it was the best solution, but he didn't like it. Not one bit. But the chance of discovery was too great. Not seeing any other alternative, he pulled the phone from his belt and handed it over.

"You're sure about this?" he asked, hoping she'd change her mind.

She nodded.

"Then scoot around to the other side of that rock. No one will see you there—unless that veil thing starts flapping in the wind like a big flag."

"It won't." She wound the lengthy material around her arm. A look of concern filled her eyes. "You will come back, won't you?"

He didn't want to. He didn't want anything to do with this mess. All he wanted was to go home and get on with his life. But he couldn't leave her sick and stranded.

"I'll be back as fast as I can."

Meghan Finnegan watched as the tailgate of the cowboy's pickup faded into the distance. The events of the day rushed up and stampeded her, knocking the air from her lungs. How could Harold have waited until she'd walked up the aisle to tell her he'd suddenly changed his mind?

He didn't want her.

And he wanted her to get rid of their unborn baby—a baby they'd agreed to keep secret until after the ceremony. Meghan wrapped her arms around her midsection. She loved her baby and she'd do whatever was necessary to care for it.

She sagged against the rock before her knees gave out. Sure, she knew Harold hadn't wanted children—he'd made that clear from the start. And with her rising television career she'd accepted that children wouldn't fit into her hectic lifestyle. But this was different—it had been an accident. When she'd told Harold about the pregnancy a few weeks ago he'd been stunned at first but then he'd seemed to accept it. What in the world had changed his mind?

The sound of an approaching vehicle—perhaps departing wedding guests—sent her scurrying behind the outcrop of large rocks. She wasn't ready to face the inquiring questions, the pitying stares or the speculative guesses. At twenty-eight, she'd prided herself on having her life all planned out. Now she was pregnant and she didn't have a clue what her next move should be.

She sank down on a small rock and yanked out scads of hairpins in order to release the veil. At last free of the yards of tulle, she ran her fingers through her hair, letting it flow over her shoulders.

She glanced down at the black phone in her lap. She should probably call her family, so they didn't worry, but there was no way she was going to deal with her mother, who would demand answers. After all, her mother had been instrumental in planning this whole affair—from setting up her initial date with the boy-next-door who'd grown up to make a fortune in the computer software business to making the wedding plans. In fact the preparations were what had finally pulled her mother out of her depression after cancer had robbed them of Meghan's father less than a year ago.

Not that all of the blame could be laid at her mother's feet. Meghan had been willing to go along with the plans—anxious to put her father's mind at ease about her future before he passed on. And, eager at last to gain her mother's hard-won approval, she'd convinced herself Harold was the man for her.

Then, as the "big day" approached the doubts had started to settle in. At first she'd thought they were just the usual bridal jitters. But Harold had started to change—to be less charming and thoughtful. It had been as though she was really seeing him for the first time. But her options had vanished as soon as the pregnancy strip displayed two little pink lines.

Meghan's hand moved to her barely-there baby bump. "It's okay, little one. Mommy will fix things. I just need some time to think."

First she had to call her family. She carefully

considered whom to contact. Her middle sister Ella? Or her little sis Katie? At the moment they weren't all that close. Since their father's death the family had splintered. She'd hoped the wedding would bring them all together again, but nothing she'd tried had worked.

Never having been very close with her youngest sister, she dialed Ella's number. The cell phone rang for a long time. Meghan had blocked Cash's number and now she worried that her sister might think it was a prank call or, worse, a telemarketer and not answer. Maybe that was for the best. She could leave a message and have no questions to field.

"Hello?" chimed Ella's hesitant voice.

"Ella, it's me. Meghan."

"Meghan—"

"Shh…don't let anyone know you're talking to me. I'm not ready to deal with Mother."

"Wait a sec." The buzz of people talking in the background grew faint, followed by the thud of a door closing. "Okay. I'm alone. What happened? Why'd you run off? Where—?"

"Slow down."

Her first instinct was to tell Ella she was stranded on the side of the road. In the past they'd shared all sorts of girly secrets—right up until Ella's engagement had ended abruptly seven months ago. Her sister hadn't been the same since then. Now, it wouldn't be right to burden her sister with her problems—not when Ella still had her own to figure out.

Meghan heard herself saying, "Don't worry. I'm fine. I'm with a friend."

"But why did you run out on the wedding? I thought you wanted to marry Harold? He acted so broken up and shocked when you took off."

"What?" Her mouth gaped as her fingers clenched the phone tighter to her ear.

"Harold barely held it together when he told the family that he didn't have a clue why you ran out on him."

"He knew…"

That low-down, sniveling, two-faced creep. Her blood boiled in her veins. How could he turn the tables on her when he was the one who'd done the jilting?

He was worried about his image. It always came back to what would look best for him and his company. Why should he take any of the blame for the ruined wedding when she wasn't there to defend herself?

"Meghan, what did he know? Are you still there?"

"He lied," she said, trying to remain calm so she didn't say something she'd regret later. But she couldn't let her sister believe Harold's lies. "He knew exactly why I left."

"It's okay," Ella said as sympathy oozed in her voice. "I understand you got cold feet. Remember I was there not that long ago—"

"I didn't get cold feet. There are things you don't know."

"Then tell me."

"I can't yet. This is different from when you called off your engagement. And it seems to me you've been spending all of your time hiding in your bakery."

"This isn't about me." Ella sighed. "Harold hinted that the stress of planning such a large wedding might have driven you over the edge."

"But that's not what happened." Why hadn't she seen this side of Harold a long time ago? Had it been there all along? She'd thought he was honorable and with time he would accept the baby.

"It doesn't matter. Just come home. The whole family is worried. Mother is beside herself. She says she'll never be able to step outside again because she's too embarrassed."

"And what do you expect me to do?" she asked, tired of being the oldest and the one expected to deal with their mother. "Nothing I say will make her less embarrassed."

In fact it'd only make it that much worse when her strait-laced mother, a pillar of the community, found out her unwed daughter was pregnant by the boy-next-door—the same guy who'd dumped her and their baby at the altar.

"But, Meghan, you have to—"

"No, I don't. Not this time. You and Katie are going to have to deal with her. I need some space to figure things out. Until I do, I won't be of any help to anyone."

Ella huffed. "So when are you coming home?"

She wanted to go to her apartment and hide away, but she wouldn't have any peace there. And there was no way she was going to her mother's house.

"I don't know. I have two weeks planned for the honeymoon so don't expect to see me before then. I'm sorry, Ella. I've got to go."

There was nothing left to say—or more like nothing she was willing to say at this point. She knew Ella was worried and frustrated, but her sister was smart and had a good head on her shoulders. She'd figure out how to manage their mother.

As Meghan disconnected the call her concern over her family was replaced by nagging doubts about the cowboy returning for her. She glanced down at the new-looking phone with a photo of a horse on the display. Surely he wouldn't toss aside his phone with his photos and numbers inside?

He'd be back…

But then again she'd put her faith in Harold and look where that had gotten her. Pregnant and alone. Her hand moved to spread across her abdomen. She'd barely come to terms with the fact there was a baby growing inside her, relying on her. And she'd already made such a blunder of things.

CHAPTER TWO

CASH ARRIVED AT the church in time to witness the groom taking his moment in the spotlight, blaming everything on Meg in order to gain the public's sympathy.

The nerve of the man amazed Cash. Meg was distraught to the point of being physically ill, and here was Harold posing for pictures. His bride might have walked out on him, but Harold sure didn't look like the injured party. A niggling feeling told him there was more to this story than the bride getting cold feet.

Ten minutes passed before he pried Gram away from consoling the groom's family and ushered her to his pickup. At last they hit the road. Gram insisted on regaling him with the tale of how the bride ran out of the church without explanation and all the wild speculations. Cash let her talk. All too soon she would learn the facts for herself.

When he reached the two-lane highway he

had only one mission—to tramp the accelerator and get back to the sickly bride. By now she must think he'd forgotten her.

Nothing could be further from the truth.

"Cash, slow down," Gram protested. "I don't know what you're in such an all-fired-up rush for. There's nothing at the Tumbling Weed that can't wait."

"It's not the ranch I'm worried about."

He could feel his grandmother's pointed gaze. "You aren't in some kind of trouble again, are you?"

He sighed, hating how his past clung to him tighter than wet denim. "Not like you're thinking."

He glanced down at the speedometer, finding he was well beyond the limit. He eased his boot up on the accelerator. As his speed decreased his anxiety rose. It was bad enough having to leave Meg alone, but when she didn't feel well it had to be awful for her.

At last he flipped on his turn signal and pulled off the road.

"What are we stopping for? Is there something wrong with the truck? I told you we should have gassed up before leaving town."

"The truck's fine."

"Then why are we stopping in the middle of nowhere? Cash, have you lost your mind?"

"Wait here." He jumped out of the truck and rushed over to the rock.

Meg wasn't there. His chest clenched. What had happened to her? He hadn't seen any sign of her walking back to town. Had someone picked her up? The thought made him uneasy.

"Meg!" He turned in a circle. "Meg, where are you?" At last he spotted her, on the other side of the road. She gathered up her dirty dress and rushed across the road. "What in the world were you doing?"

"I thought if any passing vehicles had taken notice of you dropping a bride off on the side of the road, it might be wiser if I moved to another location."

It seemed as though her nerves had settled and left her making reasonable decisions. "Good thinking. Sorry it took me a bit to get back here. Picking up my grandmother took me longer than I anticipated—"

"Cash, who are you talking to?" Gram hollered from inside the truck.

"Don't worry," he said, "that's my grandmother. Your number-one fan."

"Really? She watches my show?"

"Don't sound so surprised. From what Gram says, you've gained quite a loyal following."

"I suppose I have. That's why the network's considering taking the show national."

So she was a rising television star. Maybe Harold hadn't been up for sharing the spotlight? Cash liked the idea of Meg being more successful and popular than a man who played up the part of an injured party to gain public sympathy.

"Cash, do you hear me?" Gram yelled, her voice growing irritated.

"We'd better not keep her waiting," he said. "If she gets it in her mind to climb out of that truck without assistance I'm afraid she'll get hurt."

Meg walked beside him. "Your truck could use a stepladder to get into."

"When I bought it my intent was to haul a horse trailer, not to have beautiful women using it as a taxi service."

He noticed how splotches of pink bloomed in her cheeks. He found he enjoyed making her blush. Obviously Harold, the stuffed shirt, hadn't bothered to lather her with compliments. No wonder she'd left him.

"Before I forget, here's your phone." She placed it in his outstretched hand. "I hope you don't mind but I called my family."

"No problem." He knew if she were his sister or daughter he'd be worried. Turning his attention to his grandmother, he said, "Meg, this is my grandmother—Martha Sullivan. Gram, this is—"

"The Jiffy Cook," Gram interjected. Her thin lips pursed together. Behind her wire-rimmed glasses her gaze darted between him and Meg. "You stole the bride. Cash, how *could* you?"

His own grandmother believed *he* was the reason the bride had run away from the church. The fact it had even crossed her mind hurt. He'd have thought Gram of all people would think better of him and not believe all those scandalous stories in the press.

Before he could refute the accusation Meg spoke up. "Your grandson has been a total gentleman. When he saw me run out of the church with the press on my trail he helped me get away without any incidents. I'm sorry if it inconvenienced you, Mrs. Sullivan."

Gram waved away her concern. "It's you I'm concerned about. Has this thing with my grandson been going on for long?"

Any color in Meg's cheeks leached away, leaving her pasty white beneath the light splattering of freckles across the bridge of her nose. "I…ah…we aren't—"

"Gram, we aren't together. In fact until she ran out of the church I'd never seen Meg before. She needed a lift and I was there. End of story. No one else knows where she is."

"My goodness, what happened? Why did you run away?" Gram pressed a bony hand to her lips, halting the stream of questions. Seconds later, she lowered her hand to her lap. "Sorry, dear. I didn't mean to be so dang nosy. Climb in here and we can give you a ride back to town."

Seeing alarm in Meg's eyes, Cash spoke up, "We can't do that, Gram."

"Well, for heaven's sake, why not? She obviously needs to get out of that filthy gown. And we sure aren't going to leave her here on the side of the road."

"I can't go home," Meg spoke up. "Not yet."

"But what about Harold?" Gram asked. "Shouldn't you let him know where you are? He looked so worried."

Meg's face grew ashen as she pressed her hand to her stomach. She turned to Cash, her eyes wide with anguish. She pushed past him and ran off.

"Meg—wait." He dogged her footsteps to a rock in the distance.

When she bent at her waist he grabbed at the white material of her dress, pulling it back for her. He'd hoped the nausea had passed, but one mention of the wedding and she was sick again.

Was she overtaken by regret about leaving old what's-his-name at the altar? Had her conscience kicked in and it was so distressing that it made her ill?

He considered telling her what he'd witnessed

when he'd gone back for Gram, but what purpose would it serve? Obviously the thought of the wrecked wedding was enough to make her sick. Knowing the man she must still love had turned on her wasn't likely to help.

When she straightened, her eyes were red and her face was still ashen. She swayed and he put a steadying arm around her waist. He had no doubt the hot sun was only making things worse.

"I'm fine," she protested in a weak voice. "There's nothing left in my stomach. Just dry heaves."

He didn't release his hold on her until he had her situated in the pickup next to his grandmother. "Gram, can you turn up the air-conditioning and aim the vents on her?"

Without a word Gram adjusted the dials while he helped Meg latch her seatbelt. Once she was secure, he shut the door and rushed over to the driver's side.

He shifted into Drive, but kept his foot on the brake. "Where can we take you, Meg?"

When she didn't answer, he glanced over to find her head propped against the window. She stared off into the distance, looking as if she'd lost her best friend and didn't know where to turn. In that instant he was transported back in time almost twenty years ago, a little boy who needed a helping hand. If it hadn't been for Gram...

"We'll take you back to the Tumbling Weed," he said, surprising even himself with the decision.

"Where?" Meg's weary voice floated over to him, reassuring him that he'd made the right decision.

"It's Cash's ranch," Gram chimed in. "The perfect place for you to catch your breath."

"I don't know." She worried her bottom lip. "You don't even know me. I wouldn't want to be an imposition."

"With there just being Cash and me living there, we could use the company. Isn't that right, Cash?"

"You live there too?" Meg looked directly at his grandmother.

Gram nodded. "So, what do you say?"

Cash wasn't as thrilled about their guest as his grandmother. Meg might be beautiful, and she might have charmed his grandmother, but she was trouble. The press wasn't going to let up until they found her. He could already envision the headlines: *Runaway Bride Stolen by Thieving Cowboy.* His gut twisted into a painful knot.

"You're invited as long as you keep your location a secret," he said, his voice unbending. "I can't afford to have the press swooping in."

"Oh, no," Meg said, pulling herself upright with some effort. "I'd never bring them to your place. I don't want to see any of them."

Honesty dripped from her words, and a quick glance in her direction showed him her somber expression. But what if she started to feel better and decided she needed to fix her reputation? Or, worse, made a public appeal to what's-his-name to win him back?

Then again, she wouldn't be there that long. In fact it was still early in the day. Not quite lunchtime. If she rested, perhaps she'd be up to going home this evening.

Certain she'd soon be on her way, he said, "Good. Now that we understand each other, let's get moving."

The cold air from the vents of Cash's new-smelling pickup breathed a sense of renewed energy into Meghan. She was exhausted and dirty, but thankfully her stomach had settled. She gazed out the window as they headed southeast. She'd never ventured in this direction, but she enjoyed the vastness of the barren land, where it felt as if she could lose herself and her problems.

Instinctively she moved her hand to her stomach. There wasn't time for kicking back and losing herself. This wasn't a vacation or a spa weekend. This was a chance to get her head screwed on straight, to figure out how to repair the damage to her life and prepare to be a single mother.

The thought of her impending motherhood filled her with anxiety. What she didn't know about being a good parent could fill up an entire library. The only thing she *did* know was that she didn't want to be like her own mother— emotionally distant and habitually withholding her approval. Instead, Meghan planned to lavish her baby with love.

But what if she failed to express her love? What if she fell back on the way she'd been raised?

"Here we are," Cash announced, breaking into her troubled thoughts.

The truck had stopped in front of a little whitewashed house with a covered porch and two matching rocking chairs. The place was cute, but awfully small. Certainly not big enough for her to keep out of everyone's way.

Cash cut the engine and rounded the front of the truck. He swung open the door she'd only moments ago been leaning against. She released her seat restraint as Cash held out his hands to help her down. As the length of her dress hampered her movements she accepted his offer. His long, lean fingers wrapped around her waist.

Holding her securely, he lowered her to the ground in one steady movement.

She tilted her chin upward and for the first time noticed his towering height. Even with her heels on he stood a good six inches taller than her own five-foot-six stature. His smoky gray eyes held her captive with their intensity.

She swallowed. "Thank you."

"You're welcome." His lips lifted in a small smile, sending her tummy aflutter.

Before she could think of anything to say he turned to his grandmother and helped her out of the vehicle. Martha rushed up the walk, appearing not to need any assistance getting around. Meghan could only hope to be so spry when she got on in years.

Martha, as though remembering them, stopped on the porch. "See you at five o'clock for dinner."

She'd turned for the door when Cash said, "Wait, Gram. You're forgetting Meg."

"Not at all. She's invited too." She reached for the doorknob.

"But, Gram, aren't you going to invite her in?"

Martha turned and gave him a puzzled look. "Sure, she's welcome. But I thought she'd want to get cleaned up and changed into something fresh."

"Wouldn't she need to go inside?"

Martha's brows rose. "Um…Cash…you're going to have to take her to the big house."

"But I thought—"

"Remember after you built the house we converted your old room into my sewing room? She could sleep on the couch, but I think she'd be much more comfortable in one of your guestrooms."

This wasn't what Meghan had imagined. She'd thought they'd all be staying in one house together. The thought of staying alone with Cash sent up warning signals.

"I don't want to be a burden on either of you. If you could let me use your phone, I can call and get a ride."

Cash shot her a puzzled look. "I thought you didn't have any other place to hide from the press?"

"I don't." She licked her dry lips. Softly she added, "I'll just have to tell them…"

"What? What will you tell them?"

Panic paralyzed the muscles in her chest. "I don't know."

"Why *did* you run out on your wedding?" His unblinking gaze held hers, searching for answers.

"I…ah…"

"Why *did* you abandon the groom at the altar? Do you want him back?"

She glared at Cash. "I'm not ready to talk about it. Why are you being so mean?"

"Because that is just a small taste of what's waiting for you. In fact, this is probably mild compared to the questions they'll lob at you."

"What would a cowboy know about the press?" she sputtered, not wanting to admit he was right.

"Trust Cash," Martha piped up. "He knows what he's talking about—"

"Gram, drop it. Meg obviously doesn't want to hear our thoughts."

Meghan turned her gaze to Cash, waiting for him to finish his grandmother's cryptic comment. She'd already had her fiancé dupe her into believing he was going to marry her—that he cared about her. But if he had he wouldn't have uttered those words at the altar. Everything she'd thought about their relationship was a lie. And she wouldn't stand for one more man lying to her.

"What aren't you saying?" she demanded. "What do you know about the press?"

His jaw tensed and a muscle twitched in his cheek. His hands came to rest on his sides as his weight shifted from one foot to the other.

"I'll let you two talk," Martha said. "I've got some things to do."

The front door to the little house swished open, followed by a soft thud as it closed. All the while Meghan's gaze never left Cash. What in the world had made her think coming here was a good idea?

"I'm waiting." The August sun beat down on her in the layers of tulle and satin, leaving it clinging to her skin. Perspiration trickled down her spine. She longed to rub away the irritating sensation, but instead she stood her ground. She wouldn't budge until this stubborn cowboy told her what his cryptic comments meant.

Cash sighed. "I overheard your fiancé talking to the press and it sounded like you'll have a lot of explaining to do."

He'd turned the conversation around on her without bothering to explain his grandmother's comment. But Meghan didn't have time to point this out. She was reeling from the knowledge that Harold had not only gone to her family and blamed her for the wrecked wedding, but he'd also gone to the press with his pack of lies too. The revelation hit her like a sucker punch.

"Why would he do that?" she muttered. Her public persona was her livelihood. Was he trying to wreck her career?

"Maybe if you talked to him you could straighten things out."

She shook her head. At last she was seeing

past Harold's smooth talk and fancy airs to the self-centered man beneath the designer suits. "He doesn't want to hear what I have to say. Not after what happened."

Cash's gaze was filled with questions, but she wasn't up for answering them. Right about now she would gladly give her diamond ring just to have a shower and a glass of ice-cold water.

"Could we get out of the sun?" she asked.

Cash's brows rose, as though he'd realized he'd forgotten his manners. "Sure. My house isn't far down the lane."

Alone with this cowboy. It didn't sound like a good idea. In fact, it sounded like a really bad idea. She eyed him up. He looked reasonable. And his grandmother certainly seemed to think the sun revolved around him. So why was she hesitating? It wasn't as if she was moving in. She would figure out a plan and be out of his way in no time.

"You're safe," he said, as though reading her thoughts. "If you're that worried about being alone with me, you heard my grandmother— you can sleep on her couch. Although, between you and me, it's a bit on the lumpy side."

His teasing eased the tenseness in her stomach. He'd been a gentleman so far. There was no reason to think he'd be a threat.

As she stood there, contemplating how to

climb up into the passenger seat again, Cash said, "Let me give you a hand."

She knew without having any money or her own transportation she was beholden to him, but that didn't mean she had to give up every bit of self-reliance.

"Thanks, but I've got it." She took her time, hiking up her dress in one hand while bracing the other hand on the truck frame. With all of her might she heaved herself up and into the seat without incident. While he rounded the vehicle she latched her seatbelt.

"The lane," as he'd referred to the two dirt ruts, contained a series of rocks and potholes, and Meghan was jostled and tossed about like a rag doll.

"Did you ever consider paving this?" She clutched the door handle and tried to remain in her seat.

A deep chuckle filled the air. The sound was warm and thick, like a layer of hot fudge oozing down over a scoop of ice cream—both of which she could easily enjoy on a regular basis. Ice cream had always been something she could take or leave, but suddenly the thought of diving into a sundae plagued her, as did pulling back the layers of this mysterious cowboy.

In the next instance she reminded herself that she didn't have the time nor the energy to figure him out—not that she had any clue about men. She'd thought she'd understood Harold. The idea of being a parent must have scared him—especially since he'd never planned on having kids. It scared her too. They could have talked about it. Supported each other. But for him to cut and run at the last minute, leaving her all alone to deal with this… That was unforgivable.

She'd been so wrong about him.

And that was the real reason she found herself at this out-of-the-way ranch. If she'd been so wrong about Harold she didn't trust herself to make any more big decisions.

She glanced over at Cash. Had she been wrong to trust him?

She smothered a groan. This was ridiculous. She was overthinking everything now. She wondered if this cowboy had ever questioned his every decision. She studied the set of his strong jaw and the firm line of his lips—everything about him said he was sure of himself.

He turned and their gazes connected. His slate-gray eyes were like walls, holding in all his secrets. What kind of secrets could this rugged cowboy have?

CHAPTER THREE

CASH PULLED TO a stop in front of his two-story country home and none too soon. Meg was giving him some strange looks—not the kind he experienced from the good-time girls in the local cowboy bar. These looks were deeper, as though she had questions but didn't know how to phrase them. Whatever she wanted to know about him, he was pretty certain he didn't want to discuss it.

This ranch had become his refuge from the craziness of the rodeo circuit, and now he couldn't imagine living anywhere else. Here at the Tumbling Weed he could be himself and unwind. Though the house had been built a few years ago, he'd never brought home any female friends. He didn't want any misunderstandings. He made it known that he was a no-strings-attached cowboy. Period.

"Thanks for everything," Meg said, breaking into his thoughts. "If you hadn't helped me I don't know what I'd have done."

"I'm certain you would have made do. You don't seem like the type of person who goes long without a plan." When she didn't say anything, he glanced over. She'd bitten down on her lower lip. "Hey, I didn't mean anything by the comment. You're welcome here until you feel better."

"I don't want to get in the way."

"Have you looked at this house?" He pointed through the windshield. "I guess I got a little carried away when I had the plans drawn up. Tried to talk Gram into moving in but she flat-out refused. She said all of her memories were in her little house and she had no intention of leaving it until the good Lord called her home."

"Your grandmother sounds like a down-to-earth lady."

"She is. And the best cook around."

He immediately noticed Meg's lips purse. He'd momentarily forgotten *she* was some kind of cook. He'd bet his prize mare that Meg's scripted cooking couldn't come close to his grandmother's down-home dishes, but he let the subject drop.

Meg reached for the door handle. "Before I leave I'd love to hear about some of her recipes."

He'd met women before who only had one

thing on their minds—what they could freely gain from somebody else. He didn't like the thought of the Jiffy Cook using his grandmother's recipes to further her career. If he had his way that would never happen. And the sooner he got her settled, the sooner she'd be rested and on her way.

"Shall we go inside? I'll see if I can find something for you to change into."

"That would be wonderful. Every girl dreams about their wedding dress, but they never realize how awkward it can be to move in."

"I couldn't even imagine."

He rushed around the truck, but by the time he got there Meg had already jumped out. Seemed she'd gotten the hang of rustling up her dress to get around. The woman certainly had an independent streak. What had convinced her to chain herself to Harold?

Love. That mythical, elusive thing women wanted so desperately to believe in. He refused to buy into hearts and Valentines. There was no such thing as undying love—at least not the romantic kind. His parents' marriage should have been proof enough for him, but he'd given it a shot and learned a brutal lesson he'd never forget.

He led Meg up the steps to the large wraparound porch. This was his favorite spot in the whole house. Weather permitting, this was where he had his mid-morning coffee, and in the evening he liked to kick back to check out the stars.

"This is really nice," she said, as though agreeing with his thoughts.

"Nothing better than unwinding and looking out over the pasture."

"You're lucky to have so much space, and this view is awesome. How big is the ranch?"

"A little more than sixteen hundred acres. Plenty of room to go trail riding."

"It's like having your own little country."

He chuckled. She'd obviously spent too much time in the city. "It's not quite that big. But it's my little piece of heaven." He moved to the door and opened it. "Ready to get out of that dress?"

Color infused her cheeks and she glanced away. He tightened his jaw, smothering his amusement over her misinterpretation of his words.

Meg kept her head down and examined the dirt-stained skirt. "Shame that all it's good for now is the garbage."

"Why would you want to keep a dress from a wedding you ran away from?"

A flicker of surprise showed in her eyes and then it was gone. "If you would show me where to go, I'll get out of your way."

"The bedrooms are upstairs."

She stepped toward the living room and peered inside. "This is so spacious. And the woodwork is beautiful."

Her compliment warmed his chest, and whatever he'd been meaning to say floated clean out of his head. This was the first time he'd shown any woman other than Gram around the house he'd helped design and build. He noticed how Meg's appreciative gaze took in the hardwood floors, the built-in bookcases and the big bay window with the windowseat.

Why in the world did her words mean so much to him? It wasn't as if they were involved and he was out to impress her. She was merely a stranger passing through his life.

"I'll show you upstairs," he said, anxious for a little distance. "I'm sure I'll have something you can change into. Might not fit, but it'll be better than all of that fluff."

"I'm sorry to put you to such bother. If you are ever in Albuquerque you should look me up. The least I can do is take you to dinner." She followed him to the staircase. "Didn't you say your grandmother is a fan of the Jiffy Cook?"

He stopped on the bottom step and turned. What was she up to? He hesitated to answer, but the twinkle in Meg's eyes drew him in. "She watches the show religiously. That's why she was thrilled to get an invite to the wedding."

"So why didn't you attend? You could have gone as her escort."

His gaze moved to the floor. "I don't do weddings."

"Is that from personal experience?"

His hands clenched. What was it with this woman, making him think about things he'd rather leave buried in the dark shadows of his mind? Refusing to reveal too much, he said, "Marriage is for dreamers and suckers. Eventually people figure out there's no happily-ever-after, but by then it's usually too late."

"You can't be serious! I've never heard such a cynical view on marriage. And especially from someone who has never even tried it."

"Don't always have to try something to know it's a sham."

He didn't want to go any further with this conversation. He didn't want to think about the kids of those unhappy marriages that had no voice—no choice.

He turned his back and started up the stairs. Not hearing her behind him, he stopped to glance over his shoulder. She remained in the foyer and shot him a pitying look that pierced his chest.

"That's the saddest thing I've ever heard anyone say."

He knew better than to discuss romance and marriage with a woman. He'd thought a runaway bride would have a different perspective on the whole arrangement, but apparently today hadn't been enough to snuff out her foolish childhood fairytales.

"There's no such thing as Cinderella or happily-ever-after." He turned and climbed the rest of the stairs, certain she would follow him with that silly dejected look on her face as if he'd just told her there was no tooth fairy or Easter bunny.

Her heels clicked up the hardwood steps. There was a distinct stamp to her footsteps, as though she resented him pointing out the obvious to her. True, she had had a hard day, but what was he supposed to do? Lie to her? He didn't believe in romance. Plain and simple.

"Let's get you settled," he said, coming to a stop in the hallway. "Then we'll see about grabbing some chow…if you're up to it?"

"Actually, I'm feeling better now. And something to eat does sound good."

He opened the door and stepped back to let her pass.

"Is this your room?" she asked. "I don't want to put you out."

"No. Mine's at the other end of the hallway. This happens to be the only other bedroom I've gotten around to furnishing."

"You decorated this?" Her eyes opened wide as she began inspecting the green walls with the white crown molding.

"It isn't anything great, but I figured if I was going to have a shot at talking Gram into moving in here she might be persuaded by a cheerful room."

"It's definitely cheerful. You did a great job. And I just love the sleigh bed. It's so big you could get lost in it."

He nearly offered to come find her, but he caught himself in time. Apparently Meg's thoughts had roamed in the same direction as color flared in her cheeks and she refused to meet his gaze.

He smiled and propped his shoulder against the doorjamb. "This room has its own bathroom, so feel free to get cleaned up. I'll go find you something to change into. I'll be back."

"Thanks. Seems like I've been saying that a lot. But I mean it. I don't know what I'd have done if you hadn't been at the church."

One minute she was strong and standing her ground and the next she was sweet and vulnerable. She left his head spinning.

"I'll get those clothes."

He slipped into the hallway and strode to his bedroom. What in the world was he supposed to give her to wear? There really wasn't that much to her. She was quite a few inches shorter than him. And he recalled spying high heels when she lifted her dress.

Then there was her waist. She wasn't skinny, but still none of his pants would even come close to fitting. Not even if they were cinched up with a belt. No, he'd have to think of something else.

Cash rummaged through his closet but found nothing suitable. Then he started sorting through his chest of drawers. He made sure to dig to the bottom, hoping to find something he'd forgotten about. He couldn't believe he was doing all of this for a woman who was obviously still in love with what's-his-face. Cash's hands clenched tight around the T-shirt he'd been holding.

So, if she still loved this guy, why had she run out of the church? He was tired of contemplating that question—he resolved to try again and ask her straight up what had happened. Get it out in the open. Once he understood he'd… he'd give her advice—you know, from a guy's perspective.

With a plan in mind, he grabbed a pair of drawstring shorts and a T-shirt. He knew she'd swim in them but it was the best he could do.

He returned to the guestroom and found the door shut. He rapped his knuckles against the wood. "Meg?" He waited a few seconds. Nothing. "Meg? It's me."

He didn't hear anything. Guessing she'd opted for a shower, he decided to leave the clothes on the bed before heading down to the kitchen to scrounge up some food.

With a twist of the doorknob he swung the door open and stepped inside. His gaze landed on Meg sprawled over the bed and he came to an abrupt halt. What in the world?

She was lying on her stomach in nothing more than white thigh-high stockings, a garter belt and lacy bikini panties that barely covered her creamy backside...

He swallowed hard and blinked. The sexy vision was still there. He shouldn't be here, but his feet refused to cooperate.

A soft sigh escaped her lips, snapping him from the trance. He dropped the clothes on the cedar chest at the end of the bed and hightailed it out of the room. The image of her draped over the bed would forever be tattooed on his memory.

CHAPTER FOUR

MEGHAN SHOT UPRIGHT in bed. Something had startled her out of sleep. Her heart pounded in her chest. She shoved the flyaway strands back from her face and looked around. Where was she? Her gaze skimmed over the unfamiliar surroundings.

A knock sounded at the door. "Meg, it's dinnertime. Gram's expecting us."

The male voice was familiar. Cash. Flashes of the day's events came rushing back to her.

The wedding that would never be.

The narrow escape from the press.

Being sick on the side of the road.

And, lastly, her ride home with Cash and his grandmother.

Thanks to him she was safe. Her breath settled as the beating of her heart eased to a steady rhythm.

An insistent pounding on the door ensued. "Meg? Are you okay? If you don't answer me I'm coming in."

She glanced down at her scant bra and white lace panties. "I'm fine."

"You sure?"

"I fell asleep." She leaned over and grabbed the quilt she'd turned down earlier. With it snug over her shoulders, she was prepared in case Cash charged into the room.

"It's getting late." His deep voice rumbled through the door. "We should get moving."

Her bedraggled wedding dress lay in a heap on the floor. She never wanted to put that dress back on, but she couldn't go around wrapped in this quilt either, no matter how pretty she found the mosaic of pastel colors.

She worried at her bottom lip. Her gaze slipped to the window, where the sinking sun's rays glimmered. "But I don't have anything to wear."

"I left a few things on the cedar chest."

Relief eased the tension in her body. "Thanks. Give me five minutes to get changed."

She waited for his retreating footsteps before scrambling out from beneath the quilt. She couldn't believe she'd fallen asleep for—what? The whole afternoon? For the past couple of weeks if she hadn't been sick, she'd been tired. She wondered if it was the stress of the wedding or the baby. She pressed her hand protectively to her abdomen.

She rushed into the bathroom to wash up. When she'd finished, she stared in the mirror at her fresh-faced reflection. She had a rule about never going in public without her make-up—but that was before her life ran straight off the rails. The time had come to rethink some of those rules.

Back in the bedroom, she found the clothes where Cash had said he'd left them. Her face warmed as it dawned on her that he would have had to enter the bedroom—while she was sprawled across the bed in the lingerie she'd planned to wear on her wedding night.

The thought of the sexy giant checking her out sent a tingle of excitement zinging through her chest. A part of her wondered what he had been thinking when he realized she'd stripped down to her skivvies before sleep claimed her. Yet in the very next second a blaze of embarrassment rushed up from her chest and singed the roots of her hair—he'd seen her practically naked. Could this day get any worse?

She gave herself a mental shake and gathered the borrowed clothes. His earthy scent clung to the shirt. Her mind conjured up thoughts of the tall, muscular cowboy. If circumstances were different—if her plans were different—she wouldn't mind moving in for an up close and personal whiff of the man.

As quickly as the notion occurred to her she dismissed it. She didn't have room in her messed-up life to entertain thoughts about men. Right now she should be concentrating on more important matters, like trying to figure out her future. She had to make careful plans for the little baby growing inside her.

Not wanting to keep Cash waiting longer than necessary, she slipped on the clothes. Though the shorts and T-shirt were about five sizes too big for her, they were at least clean, and much cooler than the tattered dress she'd attempted to shove in the wastebasket.

In the bathroom, she gave her appearance a quick once-over, knowing there was no way she could make herself look good—presentable would have to do. She rushed to the top of the stairs and glanced down to where Cash was pacing in the foyer. His handsome face was creased as though he were deep in thought—probably about how soon she'd be gone from his life.

Her empty stomach rumbled. After only some juice and toast early that morning, her body was running on empty. She started down the steps.

Cash stopped and turned but didn't speak. She paused on the bottom step as his intense perusal of her outfit made her stomach flutter. Was he remembering what he'd seen upstairs when she'd been sleeping? For a moment she wondered if he'd liked the view.

She forced a tentative smile. "Ready to eat?"

He didn't return her friendly gesture. In fact, his face lacked any visible emotion. "I've been ready."

"Do you always eat at your grandmother's?"

He shifted his weight. "With it just being me here, and Gram all alone, I like to keep tabs on her. Sharing meals allows me to make sure she's okay without it seeming like I'm checking up on her. Speaking of which, we'd best get a move on."

Meghan glanced down and wiggled her freshly manicured, pink-painted toes. "I don't have any shoes."

He sighed. "Wait here. I think I have something that'll work."

She couldn't imagine what he'd have that would fit her size seven feet. A glance at his impressive cowboy boots confirmed her feet would be lost in anything he wore.

When Cash returned from the kitchen he was toting a couple of large bags. He stopped in front of her and dropped them at her feet. "Take a look in those."

Confused, she peeked inside, finding both bags full of clothes of varying colors. "I don't understand. Where did these come from?"

"This afternoon Gram needed some stuff in town. So while you were napping I drove her. We picked up some essentials. Whatever doesn't fit can be returned or exchanged."

Her mouth gaped. She wasn't used to such generosity. Harold had always been a stickler for keeping their expenses separate. At first she'd found it strange, but she didn't mind paying her own way. In fact she'd soon learned she liked being self-reliant and the freedom that came with it.

"But I can't accept these," she protested.

Cash frowned. "Why not?"

"I don't have any money to pay you back... at least not on me."

"It's okay. I can afford it."

She shook her head. "I didn't mean that. It's just you hardly know me and you've already opened your home up to me. I can't have you buying me clothes too."

His brow arched. "Are you sure that's the only reason? After all, they aren't designer fashions."

"I'm not a snob. Just because I'm on television doesn't mean I'm uppity—"

"Fine." He held up his palms to stop her litany. "Consider this a loan. You can pay me back when you get home."

The idea appealed to her. She really didn't have too many options. "It's a deal."

She bent down and dug through the bag until her fingers wrapped around a pair of bubble-gum-colored flip-flops. A little big for her, but it didn't matter. They fit well enough and they'd be cool in this heat. Double win.

Outside, he held open the truck door for her. She really wanted to walk and enjoy the fresh air and scenery but, recalling they were running late, she didn't mention it. Suddenly her plans to flee this ranch as soon as possible didn't seem quite so urgent. This little bit of heaven was like a soothing balm on her frazzled nerves. In fact Cash was making her feel right at home.

The bumps on the way to his grandmother's house didn't bother her so much this time, and thankfully it didn't kick up her nausea. She was feeling better after that nap. Amazing how sleep could make a new person out of you.

Cash pulled to a stop and turned to her. "Before you go inside, I know you're a fancy cook and all, but my grandmother is a simple woman with simple tastes. She's proud of her abilities. Don't make her feel bad if her food isn't up to your TV standards."

It hurt that he'd immediately assumed she'd be snooty about dinner. She might be on TV, but she loved home-cooking the same as the next guy.

Heck, if Cash knew she was pregnant and the

father had dumped her on her keester, he probably wouldn't worry so much. However, she had no intention of telling him her little secret. He'd already witnessed her at her lowest point—she wasn't about to confirm that her entire life was completely out of control.

"I'd never say or do anything to upset your grandmother. I'm very grateful for her kindness."

"You swear?"

She blinked. He didn't trust her? "I promise."

He eyed her, as if to discern if she were on the level. Apparently she passed his test because he climbed out of the truck and she met him on the sidewalk.

The fact he didn't trust her without even giving her a chance bothered her. Why did he seem so wary of her? Because she was on television? What did he have against TV personalities? Or was it something else?

She most likely wouldn't be here long enough to figure it out. After she'd had something to eat she'd think up her next move. Yet it made her cringe to think of facing her mother and telling her that she was pregnant and the father didn't want her or the baby.

Cash trailed Meg into his grandmother's house. Even the sweet sashay of her rounded backside wasn't enough to loosen the unease in his chest. In fact it made the discomfort worse.

His mind filled with visions of her bare limbs sprawled across the bed while her assets were barely covered with the sheerest material. It'd taken every bit of willpower to quietly back out of the room and shut the door. No woman had a right to look that tantalizing without even trying.

He couldn't believe he was letting her get to him. He thought he'd become immune to feminine charms. Take them or leave them had been his motto. And the way this little redhead could distract him with her shapely curves and heart-stopping smile were sure signs he should leave her alone.

"Remember what we talked about," he said.

"I'm not a child. You don't have to keep reminding me—like I'd *ever* be so rude."

"Good."

He followed her up the steps to the porch. He wanted to believe Meg, but he'd been lied to by his straight-faced ex-girlfriend. In his experience, when women wanted something badly enough they could be sneaky and deceptive. Now he preferred to err on the side of caution.

After all, Gram had been preparing for this meal ever since they'd returned from town. It'd only take one wrong look or word from the Jiffy

Cook, his grandmother's favorite television celebrity, and Gram would be crushed.

Cash rapped his knuckles on the door of the modest four-room house before opening it and stepping inside. "Gram, we're here. And, boy, does something smell good."

His grandmother came rushing out of the kitchen wearing a stained apron, wiping her hands on a towel. "Good. I threw together a new dish. I hope you both like it."

"I'm starved," Meg said.

"Okay, you two go wash up. Cash can show you to the bathroom."

He nodded, then led the way. In silence, they lathered up. Even standing next to her, doing the most mundane thing, he couldn't relax. Every time he glanced her way he started mentally undressing her until she had nothing on but that sheer white underwear. His throat tightened and he struggled to swallow.

What was wrong with him? He barely even knew her, and he had absolutely no intention of starting up anything. His focus needed to be on rebuilding this ranch, not daydreaming about a brief fling with the tempting redhead next to him.

Back in the kitchen, Gram said, "I'll warn you—dinner's nothing special."

Cash held back a chuckle at his grandmother's attempt to downplay this meal. He wished she'd made one of her tried-and-true dishes instead of taking a chance on something new to impress their guest. But no matter what it tasted like he would smile and shovel it in.

"What did you make?" Meg asked.

"I tried something a little different. I was hoping for your opinion."

"My opinion?" Meg pressed a hand to her chest and the light glittered off the rock on her ring finger. The wedding dress might be gone, but the impressive engagement ring remained. Obviously she wasn't quite through with what's-his-name.

"You're the expert."

Remembering his manners, he pulled out a chair for Meg. Having absolutely nothing to add to this conversation, he quietly took his usual seat.

"I'm no expert." Sincerity rang out in Meg's voice. "I just cook and I hope other people will like the same things as me."

"I'll let you in on a little secret," Gram said, leaning her head toward Meg. "I watch your show every day and I jot down the recipes I think Cash will like."

Meg leaned toward Gram and lowered her voice. "And does he like them?"

Cash wasn't so sure he liked these two women

putting their heads together to discuss him. "You two *do* remember that I'm in the room, right?"

"Of course we do." Gram sent him a playful look. "Yes, he likes them."

So now he understood why he'd been eating some strange dishes for the past year—Gram had been imitating Meg. Interesting. But he still preferred Gram's traditional recipes, such as homemade vegetable barley soup and her hearty beef stew.

"Dinner isn't quite ready," Gram said. "The shopping today put me a little behind. I have some fresh bread in the oven, and I have to add the tortellini to the soup."

"Anything I can help with?" Cash offered, as he did at each meal.

Usually she waved him off, but today she said, "Yes, you could get us some drinks."

"Drinks?" Their standard fare normally consisted of some tap water. On really hot, miserable days they added ice for something special.

"Yes. I picked up some soda and juice at the store." Gram turned to Meg. "I'm sure you're probably used to something fancy with your meals, like champagne or wine, but I'm afraid we're rather plain around here. If you want something we don't have I'll have Cash pick it up for you the next time he's in town."

"That won't be necessary. You've already

been too generous with the clothes. Thank you for being so thoughtful."

"I didn't know what you would wear, and Cash wasn't much help."

"I haven't had a chance to go through them." Pink tinged her cheeks. "I slept longer this afternoon than I'd planned...well, I hadn't planned to go to sleep at all."

"I'm sure you were worn out after such a terrible day. You poor child."

"You can help yourself to drinks," Cash said, trying to offset his grandmother's mollycoddling.

"Oh, no, she can't. She's our guest. You can serve her."

Cash swallowed down his irritation. The last thing in the world he'd wanted to do was upset his grandmother.

Gram and Meg discussed the Jiffy Cook's show while he kept himself busy. He opened the cabinet and sorted through a stack of deep bowls, trying to find ones that weren't chipped on the edges. He'd never noticed their worn condition before today. A sense of guilt settled over him like a dense fog. He'd been too focused on the rodeo circuit and hadn't paid enough attention to the small things at home. He made a mental note to get his grandmother some new dishes.

When Gram turned her back to check on the bread in the oven Meg held out her hands for the bowls. Cash handed them over. No need to stand on ceremony. It wasn't as if she was an invited guest or anything. He had no idea why Gram was treating the woman like some sort of royalty—even if her burnt-orange curls, the splattering of freckles across the bridge of her nose and the intense green eyes *were* fit for a princess.

He gathered the various items they'd need for dinner and laid them on the edge of the table. When he turned around he found Meg had set everything out accordingly. Maybe she wasn't as spoiled as he'd imagined.

Again the light caught the diamond on her hand and it sparkled, serving as a reminder of how much she liked nice things—expensive things. And, more importantly, that she was a woman who didn't take off her engagement ring after calling off the wedding—a woman with lingering feelings for her intended groom.

Cash's jaw tightened. Best not get used to having her around. After dinner he'd drive her wherever she needed to go.

Gram stirred the pot and set aside the spoon. "These are a couple of recipes that I pulled from one of my new cookbooks. Don't know how they'll turn out. If nothing else, the bread is tried and true. Cash can attest to how good it is."

"You bet. Gram makes the best fresh-baked bread in the entire county. With a dab of fresh-churned butter it practically melts in your mouth."

"You don't have to sell me on it." A smile lit up Meg's eyes. "I had a whiff of it when she opened the oven. I can't wait to eat."

"Well, if you're hungry we can start with the salad." Gram hustled over to the fridge and removed three bowls with baby greens, halved grape tomatoes and rings of red onion. "This is the first time I've made blue cheese and bacon dressing from scratch."

"Sounds good to me," Meg said. "But you know you didn't have to make anything special. Your usual recipes would have been fine."

"But those dishes aren't good enough for a professional chef."

"I'm not a chef. Just a cook—like you. And I'm sure your salad will be delicious."

Gram turned back to the fridge and pulled out a plastic-wrapped measuring cup. She moved it to the table before retrieving the whisk from the counter. In an instant she had the dressing unwrapped and was stirring the creamy mixture. Cash's mouth began to water. Okay, so maybe Gram didn't have to go to all this trouble, but he had to admit some of her experiments turned out real well, and this dinner was slated to get star ratings.

Cash passed the first bowl to Meg. He noticed how the smile slid from her face. And her eyes were huge as she stared at the salad. He wanted to tell her to drown it in black pepper—anything so she would eat it. With his grandmother by his side, he was limited to an imploring stare.

For some reason he hadn't thought a chef—or, as she called herself, a *cook*—would be opposed to blue cheese. Was it his grandmother's recipe? Had Gram made some big cooking blunder?

"Eat up, everyone." Gram smiled and sat across the table from him. "There's more if anyone wants seconds."

He immediately filled his fork and shoveled it in his mouth. The dressing was bold, just the way he liked it. But *his* impression wasn't the one that counted tonight. He cast Meg a worried glance. He couldn't let this meal fall apart. He moved his foot under the table and poked Meg's leg.

"Ouch!" Gram said. "Cash, what are you doing? Sit still."

"Sorry," he mumbled. "This is really good."

"Thank you." Gram's face lit up.

It was Meg's turn to chime in, but she didn't. Her fork hovered over the bowl. *Eat a bite,* he willed her. *Just take a bite and praise my grand-mother.*

"Excuse me." Meg's chair scraped over the wood floor and like a shot she was out of the room.

Cash inwardly groaned as he watched her run away. He turned back to find disappointment glinting in his grandmother's eyes. It didn't matter what he said now, the meal was ruined. Meg had gone and broken her word to him.

His fingers tightened around the fork. He should have listened to the little voice in his head that said not to trust a spoiled celebrity—one who hadn't even seen fit to stick around for her own wedding.

CHAPTER FIVE

A SPLASH OF cold water soothed Meghan's flushed cheeks but did nothing to ease her embarrassment. She was utterly mortified about her mad dash from the dinner table. One minute she'd felt fine, but after the stern warning from Cash to enjoy the dinner and his constant stares her stomach had twisted into a gigantic knot. The whiff of blue cheese had been her final undoing.

"Thank you for being so understanding," Meghan said, accepting a towel from Cash's grandmother.

"I've been there, child. I remember it as if it were yesterday. I was sick as a dog when I was carrying Cash's father."

"But I'm not—"

Martha silenced her with a knowing look. "Honey, there's no point trying to close the gate when the horse is obviously out of the corral."

There was no sense carrying on the charade.

Meghan sank down on the edge of the large clawfoot tub. "I wanted to keep the news to myself for now. It's the main reason I'm here. The thought of being a single mother scares me, and I need a plan before I go home."

Martha patted her hand. "I won't say a word to anyone. And you can stay here as long as you need."

"But Cash—"

"Don't worry about him. He's gruff on the outside but he's a softy on the inside."

"I don't know… He already thinks I'm spoiled and self-centered. I can't tell him about the baby and have him thinking I'm irresponsible too."

"Give my grandson another chance. He can be extremely generous and thoughtful."

To those he loves, Meghan silently added. She admired the way he looked after his grandmother. Everyone should have someone in their life who cared that much.

Where she was concerned he wasn't so generous. She was an outsider. Although she had to admit he had willingly opened his home to her, and for that she was grateful.

Feeling better, Meghan agreed to try a little of the soup. Martha looked pleased with the idea and rushed off to dish some up for her.

Meghan moved to the mirror and inspected her blotchy complexion. She looked awful and she didn't feel much better. No one had ever warned her being pregnant would feel like having a bad case of the flu. She groaned. Or was it a case of overwrought nerves? The pressure and warning looks from Cash had made her entire body tense.

She shrugged and turned away. Either way, she'd gone back on her word to him and ruined the dinner. How in the world would she make it up to him?

She eased out of the bathroom and found him pacing in the living room. "I'm really sorry about that."

His brows drew together and he gave her a once-over. "You feeling better?"

She nodded, but didn't elaborate.

"Good. But you should have told me you still didn't feel well. I wouldn't have dragged you to dinner. I would have explained it to my grandmother."

Meghan eyed him. Was this the cowboy's way of apologizing for those death stares at the dinner table? The tension in her stomach eased. Something told her apologies, even awkward ones, didn't come easily to him.

"Apology accepted. But I was feeling fine and then it just hit me at once. I told Martha I would try a little broth and bread. Have you finished eating?"

"No."

"Sorry for disturbing everyone's dinner. If you want, we can try again."

On her way back to the kitchen her gaze roamed over the house, admiring all the old pieces of oak furnishing. Everything was in its place, but a layer of dust was growing thick. Definitely not the perfect home appearance her mother had instilled in Meghan. Her mother had insisted that the perfect house led to the perfect life and the perfect future. This motto had been drilled into her as a child. If only life was that easy.

She worried about how she'd scar her own child. How in the world would she instill confidence in them? Especially when she struggled daily with the confidence to follow her own dreams?

"You sure you're okay?" Cash asked just outside the kitchen.

"Yes, I'm fine."

She really should level with him about her pregnancy, but she couldn't bring herself to broach the subject. She didn't want him to look down at her—a single woman, dumped at the altar by her baby's daddy as if he was tossing out a carton of sour milk.

Definitely not up for defending herself, she stuck with her decision to keep her condition to herself. Besides, it was none of his business. Soon she'd be gone and their paths most likely would never cross again.

With Cash acting friendly, Meghan relaxed and savored every drop of the delicious broth. She even finished every morsel of the thick slice of buttered bread. "That was delicious. I'd love to have more, but I don't think I should push my luck."

"Still not feeling a hundred percent?" Cash asked, concern reflected in his eyes.

The fact he genuinely seemed worried about her came as a surprise. "Not exactly. Would you believe I'm ready to go back to sleep again?"

He didn't say a word. Instead he kept his head lowered, as though it took all his concentration to slather butter on a slice of bread.

Martha reached out and patted her hand. "Cash can run you back to the house so you can rest."

His head immediately lifted. Deep frown lines bracketed his eyes and lips.

"I don't want to overstay my welcome," Meghan said. She wasn't sure what alternatives she had, but she'd come up with something. "If you could just give me a lift to the closest town."

Was that a flicker of relief that she saw reflected in his eyes? She'd thought they'd made peace with each other, but perhaps she'd been mistaken.

As though oblivious to the undercurrent of tension, his grandmother continued. "Nonsense. You barely made it through dinner. You're in no condition to go home and face those reporters. Cash knows all about how merciless they can be. Isn't that right, Cash?"

His blank stare shifted between his grandmother and herself. He merely nodded before dunking his bread in the remaining soup in his bowl.

Meghan couldn't stay where she wasn't wanted. If Cash wouldn't set his grandmother straight she'd have to do it herself. "But I can't…"

Martha's steady gaze caught hers. The woman quietly shook her head and silenced her protest. Maybe the woman had a point. Stress definitely exacerbated the unease in her stomach. But if Cash didn't want her, where would she spend the night? She'd already eyed up Martha's small couch with its uneven cushions. Her back hurt just from looking at it.

"So how long can you stay?" Martha asked.

"I do have two weeks of vacation time planned. It was supposed to be for my honeymoon."

"Well, there you have it. Plenty of time to rest up. We'll make your stay here as pleasant as possible." Martha got to her feet. "Cash can drive you back to his place."

Cash looked none too happy with his grandmother's meddling. "I will as soon as the kitchen is straightened up."

This wasn't right. She didn't want them going out of their way for her. "I'll stay on one condition."

His brow arched. "And what would that be?"

"I refuse to be waited on. I want to do my share—starting with cleaning the dinner dishes."

He shrugged. "Fine by me. I don't have time to wait on you with a ranch to run."

She nodded, understanding that he had his hands full. "I think your grandmother should go in the living room and put up her feet after she's slaved away all afternoon making this fantastic meal."

The older woman's gaze moved back and forth between her and her grandson. Meghan braced herself for an argument. She might be down and out right now, but that didn't mean she was utterly pathetic and in need of being waited on hand and foot.

"Thank you." Martha started for the doorway. "There's a classic movie on tonight and I don't want to miss it."

The woman slipped off her sunflower-covered apron and hustled out of the room without a backward glance.

Cash's gray eyes filled with concern. "Do you think she's okay?"

"I don't really know her, but she seems okay to me. Why do you ask?"

"It's not like her to leave the work to others. She's normally a very stubborn woman who won't rest until the house is in order."

During the meal, Meghan had noticed the kitchen needed some sprucing up, and the windows needed to be wiped down inside and out. Maybe his grandmother needed some help around the place. A plan formed in her mind as to how she could carry her weight while at the Tumbling Weed and keep from dwelling too much on her problems.

"Maybe she figured there was enough help in the kitchen and she wasn't needed. I wouldn't worry. Just be glad she's taking a moment to rest. She deserves it."

"She certainly does. I've tried to get her to slow down for years now, but instead I think she does more. Heck, a lot of days she invites the ranch hands to the house for lunch. And then she fights with me when I insist on helping with the clean-up. And when any of the neighbors need a helping hand she's the first to volunteer, whether it's to cook for another family or to care for a sick person."

"Your grandmother is amazing. I wish I still had my grandmothers, but one died before I was born and the other passed on when I was in grade school."

"Gram is definitely a force to be reckoned with. Maybe you can help keep an eye on her while you're here? Make sure there's nothing wrong? As you can tell, I'm not good at reading women. I had no idea that you were still sick." He glanced down, avoiding her stare. "I thought you didn't like my grandmother's cooking."

She glanced over her shoulder to make sure they were alone and then lowered her voice so as not to be overheard. "Actually, I was going to suggest that I could earn my keep by being housekeeper and helping with the cooking. I'm thinking it's been a while since your grandmother's house has been washed top to bottom, so I could clean here. It would give me something to do all day."

"I don't know."

She pursed her lips together and counted to ten. "I'm not some spoiled actress. I'm a local television cook. Period. I still do everything for myself."

He stepped closer. "Then I'd say you have yourself a job. Do as much as Gram will let you."

With him standing right in front of her, she was forced to crane her neck to meet his gaze. When he wasn't scowling at her he really was quite handsome, with those slate-gray eyes, a prominent nose, stubble layering his tanned cheeks and a squared jaw.

And then there was his mouth. She found herself staring at his lips, wondering what his kisses would be like. Short and sweet? Or long and spicy? When his mouth bowed into a smile she lifted her gaze and realized she'd been busted. She grew uncomfortably warm, but she didn't let on.

This was a way to earn her keep and extend her time here, allowing her a chance to think. She liked the idea. This way she wouldn't feel indebted to the sexy cowboy who made her feel a little off-center when he stood so close to her—like he was doing now.

The next morning Meghan awoke to a knock. Had she slept in again? Her eyes fluttered open and she sat up in bed to find herself surrounded by darkness.

It was still the middle of the night. What in the world was going on?

"Cash, is that you?"

"Who else were you expecting?"

"No one." She yawned and stretched, enjoying the comfort of the big bed. "It must be the middle of the night."

"It won't be dark for long. You planning to sleep the day away?"

"The day? The sun hasn't even climbed out of bed."

"It'll be up before you know it. That's why a rancher has to get an early jump on the day."

Meghan groaned. "Fine. I'll be downstairs in a half hour."

"Ten minutes, tops."

"Ten?" she screeched before scrambling out of bed. The coldness from the bare wood floor seeped up her legs and shocked her sluggish body to life.

She didn't care what he said. She was getting a shower. Otherwise there was no way she'd make it through the day. She rushed into a hot steamy shower before sorting out a pair of blue jeans and a T-shirt, both of which were a little big. She supposed in her current condition that was a good thing. She pressed her hand to her almost non-existent baby bump. Shortly after she returned home she'd most likely be getting herself a whole new wardrobe—*maternity clothes, here I come.*

The assortment of supplies in the bag was quite extensive. Meghan located a hairbrush and ponytail holders. She made quick use of them, pulling her unruly curls back. Without worrying about her lack of make-up, she ran downstairs.

Cash reached for the doorknob. "It's about time."

"I hurried," she protested, still feeling a bit damp from her shower. "Especially considering it's the middle of the night."

He chuckled, warming her insides. "Hardly. Gram probably already has breakfast started."

"Well, then, lead the way. We don't want to keep her waiting." And she had a job to do—a means to earn her keep.

"Are you feeling better this morning?"

"Much better. The sleep really helped."

He studied her. "Your stomach is okay?"

She nodded, touched by his concern. "In fact I'm ravenous. Now, quit with the overprotective act and get moving."

He grinned at her. "Yes, ma'am."

Her empty stomach did a somersault. How could his smile do such crazy things to her insides? She refused to dwell on its meaning as she rushed to the pickup. The short ride to Martha's house was quiet. Without caffeine, Meghan lacked the energy to make idle chitchat, even though Cash's mood appeared to have improved.

When he pulled to a stop in front of the steps leading to his grandmother's house Meghan glanced over to him. "Aren't you coming inside?"

"Later. Right now I have the animals to tend to."

"But don't you need something in your stomach?"

"I had a mug of stiff black coffee while I waited for you." He patted his stomach and rubbed. "It's the fuel this cowboy runs on."

Meghan scrunched up her nose. "I never learned how to drink that stuff straight up. I always add milk and sugar."

"Gram should have everything you need to make yourself a cup. I'll see you soon. Remember our deal."

"I won't forget. Your grandmother is my first priority." She didn't want to think about her other priorities—not at this unseemly hour. "Maybe later I can help you in the barn."

"And break those pretty nails? I don't think so."

She held out her hands and for the first time noticed she was still wearing Harold's ring. She wanted to rip it from her finger and toss it out the window, but instead she balled up her hands and stuffed them back in her lap. Disposing of the ring now would only evoke a bunch of questions from Cash—questions she didn't want to answer.

"My nails aren't long. They can't be. Remember I'm a cook?"

"Long or short, you weren't born and bred to this kind of work. A pampered star like yourself will be much better off in the kitchen with my grandmother."

"I'm not pampered."

She pursed her lips together. She didn't like being told what she could and couldn't do. Harold had told her she needed to be a television personality because she was too pretty to hide in some kitchen. Looking back now, she wondered if he hadn't pushed her into taking the television spot, if she'd have chosen that career path for herself. Her love had always been for the creative side of cooking, and it rubbed her the wrong way to have recipes provided for her merely to demonstrate.

"I'll bet I can keep up with you in the barn," she said. Her pricked ego refused to back down.

He raised his cowboy hat. "You think so, huh?"

"I do."

Humor reflected in his eyes. "Maybe we'll put you to the test, but right now you're needed in the kitchen."

"I know. I haven't forgotten our deal. But that doesn't mean it's the only thing I can do."

She hopped out of the truck and sent the door swinging shut. With her hands clenched, she marched up the walk. Just because she hadn't been fortunate enough to be born into such a beautiful ranch with dozens of horses, it didn't mean she couldn't learn her way around the place.

The time had come to prove to herself that she could stand on her own two feet. With a baby on the way, she needed to know she could handle whatever challenges life threw at her.

If earning her keep meant cleaning up after this cowboy and his horses, she'd do it. After all, it couldn't be that hard—could it?

CHAPTER SIX

CASH SAT ASTRIDE Emperor, a feisty black stallion, as the mid-morning sun beat down on his back. He brought the stallion to a stop in the center of the small arena. He'd spent a good part of the morning working with this horse in preparation for its new owner.

The stallion lowered his head, yanking on the reins. Cash urged the horse forward, which in turn raised Emperor's head, allowing him to retain his hold on the reins. Cash's injured shoulder started to throb, but he refused to quit. This horse was smart and beautiful. He just needed to remember who was the boss.

They started circling the arena again. The horse's hooves thudded against the dry earth, kicking up puffs of dirt that trailed them around the small arena. With the horse at last following directions, Cash's thoughts strayed back to the redhead with the curvy figure. It wasn't the first time she'd stumbled into his thoughts. In fact she was on his mind more than he wanted to admit.

"Nice horse. Can I ride him?"

The lyrical chime of a female voice roused him from his thoughts. Cash slowed Emperor to a stop and turned. He immediately noticed Meg's pink and white cowboy hat—the one he'd picked out for her. She looked so cute—too cute for his own comfort.

She wouldn't be classified as skinny, which suited him just fine. When he pulled a woman into his arms he liked to feel more than skin and bones. But she wasn't overweight either. She was someplace between the two—someplace he'd call perfect.

His pulse climbed. All he could envision was wrapping his arms around her and seeing if her lips were as soft as they appeared.

Meghan rested her hands on the fence rail. "After that challenge you threw down this morning about how I couldn't be a cowgirl because I wasn't born on a ranch, I came to prove you wrong."

He couldn't help but chuckle at the fierce determination reflected in her green eyes. This woman was certainly a little spitfire. And at the same time he found her to be a breath of fresh air.

"You wouldn't want to ride Emperor. He can

be a handful. If you're serious, I'll find you a gentler mount." He turned Emperor loose in the pasture and joined her by the fence. "But what about our arrangement? Shouldn't you be helping my grandmother?"

"I did. After we cleaned up the breakfast dishes I ran the vacuum, even though Martha complained the entire time about how she could do it all herself. And then I dusted—before your grandmother shooed me out of the house, insisting her morning cooking shows were coming on and she didn't want to be disturbed. I'll go back and do more later."

"My grandmother does like her routines."

Meg climbed up and perched on the white rail fence. Her left hand brushed his arm as she got settled. He noticed something was different about her, but he couldn't quite figure it out—then it dawned on him. She'd taken off the flashy diamond. The urge to question her about the missing ring hovered at the back of his throat but he swallowed down his curiosity—it shouldn't matter to him.

"The horse you were riding is a beauty. You're lucky to own him."

"He isn't mine."

Her brows lifted. "He isn't?"

"No. I train horses and sell them. So technically he's mine, but only until the buyer shows up later this week to collect him."

"That must be tough. Spending so much time with the horses and then having to part with them."

He shrugged. "It's a way of life I've grown up around. You have to keep your emotions at bay when it comes to business. Now, don't get me wrong. I have my own horses and there's no way I'd part with *them*. They're family."

"I've heard about men and their horses." She eyed him speculatively.

"Yep, we're thick as thieves."

"Are you up for that ride now?" she asked.

Her jean-clad thigh had settled within an inch of his arm. It'd be so easy to turn around and nestle up between her thighs. He'd pull her close and then he'd steal a kiss from this woman whose image in lacy lingerie still taunted his thoughts.

What in the world was he thinking? He bowed his head and gave it a shake, clearing the ridiculous thoughts. It was then that he noticed her old cowboy boots. His grandmother must have lent them to her. He considered explaining how he needed to keep on working, but he liked her company—even if it were purely platonic—and he didn't want her to leave quite yet.

"I'll give you a quick tour of the ranch."

She leveled him a direct stare and then a smile tugged at those sweet lips. "I already like what I've seen."

His heart rammed into his windpipe. Meg's eyes filled with merriment as her smile broadened. Was she flirting with him? Impossible. She was only being friendly. After all, she was still hung up on what's-his-name. And that was for the best.

Cash cleared his throat, anxious to change the conversation to a safer subject. "We'll start here. This is the arena where I do a lot of work with the horses. And over there—" he pointed to an area behind the barn "—is a smaller corral where we break in the young ones."

"Can I watch you sometime?"

"Sure." He longed to show her some of his skills. He cleared his throat. "And this way leads to the barn."

Out of habit, he worked his sore shoulder in a circular motion. The persistent dull ache was still there—it was always there, sometimes better and sometimes worse. Right now it was a bit better.

"When did you hurt your shoulder?" Meg asked as she rushed to catch up with him.

He didn't like talking about that time in his life. When he'd been discharged from the hospital he'd made tracks, putting miles between him and the press. All he'd wanted to do was forget the whole scene and the events that had led up to his accident. And it wasn't something he wanted to delve into with this television personality. Sure, she was just a cook, and highly unlikely to be able to use any of the information he gave her, but she was closely linked to people who would love a chance to revisit the scandal. After all, it wasn't as if it was ancient history. It'd only happened a little more than three months ago.

He carefully chose his words. "It happened at my last rodeo in Austin."

"You're a rodeo cowboy?" A note of awe rang out in her voice.

"Not anymore. I walked away from it a few months back."

"Did your decision have something to do with your shoulder?"

He shrugged. "Maybe a little."

"What happened?"

"I made good time out of the gate, but the steer I drew stumbled during the takedown and we hit the ground together. Hard. I landed on my shoulder at exactly the wrong angle."

"Ouch." Meg winced. "Shouldn't you be resting and letting it heal?"

"I did rest after the surgery."

"Surgery? What did they have to do?"

"Pop a pin in to hold everything together. Not a big deal." He knew guys with far worse injuries, but it was best not to mention that to Meg. "I did my stint in rehab and now I'm back on horseback."

"I can't imagine loving something so much that you would take such risks."

"Don't you love being in front of the cameras, cooking up something new for your fans?"

Seconds passed, as though she were trying to make up her mind. "The fans are great. It's the rest of it that gets old. Watching what I eat because the camera puts fifteen pounds on me is pure drudgery. And it's frustrating being told what will and what won't be in each segment instead of having a voice in the show's content."

"I thought the stars were in charge?"

She shook her head. "Maybe if you're Paula Deen or Rachael Ray, but not for some no-name on a local network."

So she wasn't as big a star as his grandmother had built her up to be? Interesting. He wondered what else he had got wrong about her.

"If you were no longer a television personality, what would you do with your life?"

She paused and stared at him. Their gazes locked and his heart thump-thumped in his chest. His eyes dipped to her lips. What would it be like to kiss her? Maybe if he swooped in for a little smooch then he'd realize his imagination had blown her appeal way out of proportion.

"I...I don't know." Pink tinged her cheeks.

Could she read his mind? Was she having the same heady thoughts? Would it be so wrong to steal a kiss?

She glanced away. "Right now I'm rethinking everything. With my marriage being off, my life is about to take a very different direction, and I have to start planning what I'm going to do next."

The reminder of her almost-wedding washed away his errant desire to kiss her. She'd already run out on the guy she'd promised to marry—she was the kind of woman who'd let a man down without a second thought. And he didn't need someone like that in his life.

In no time at all Meghan was sitting astride Cinnamon, a gentle mare. Cash led her on a brief tour of the Tumbling Weed. She couldn't help but admire all the beautiful horses in the meadow, but it was the cowboy at her side that gave her the greatest pause. With his squared chin held high and his broad shoulders pulled back, he gave off a definite air of confidence. She couldn't help but admire the way he moved, as if he were one with the horse.

"Tell me a little about yourself," Cash said.

"You don't want to hear about me. You'd be bored senseless."

"Consider it part of you getting the job. After all, there'd normally be some sort of interview where I'd get to know at least the broad strokes of your life."

He had a point. If *she* had a stranger working and living with her, she'd want some background information too. But opening up about herself and her family didn't come easily to her.

Her mother had taught her to hide their family flaws and shortcomings from the light of day. And never, ever to let the man in your life know of them—not if you wanted to plan a future with him. Meghan had foolishly followed that advice with Harold and held so much of herself back. As a result they'd had a very superficial relationship.

She never wanted that to happen again. If a man was to love her, he had to see her just as she was—blemishes and all.

But that didn't make revealing her imperfections any less scary. Thankfully she could take her first plunge into honesty with a man she had no intention of getting romantically entangled with.

"Let's see—you already know I'm a professional cook. I grew up in Lomas, New Mexico. I have two younger sisters. And my parents were married almost thirty years before my father died of cancer this past winter."

"Are you close to your family?"

The easy answer teetered on the tip of her tongue, but she bit it back. The point was to learn to open up about herself. "The family splintered apart after my father died. Since I'm the oldest, I know it falls to me to keep everyone together. But too much happened too fast and I...I failed."

Seconds passed before Cash said, "I don't know about your particular situation, but in my experience I've learned some families are better off apart."

Sadness smothered her as the truth of his words descended over her. She didn't want that to be true of her family. But, more than that, she wondered what he'd lived through to come to such a dismal conclusion.

She wanted to ask. She wanted to offer him some hope. But she couldn't let herself get drawn into his problems when she had so many of her own.

Instead, she changed the subject. "How many horses do you have?"

"Fifty-one. I aim to have close to a hundred when all is said and done."

"That's a lot."

"Sure is. But with thousands of cowboys roaming through the West, and the right sort of advertising, I'm thinking soon I'll have more business than I can handle."

"Do you have a business plan?" She was curious to know if a cowboy could also have a mind for business.

"I do. Why do you ask?"

"Just curious. So, do you advertise?" She almost blurted out that she'd never heard of the Tumbling Weed before yesterday, but she caught herself in time.

"I have a website, and I've taken out ads in various publications, but the best form of advertising by far is word of mouth."

So he knew his stuff. She was impressed. She had a feeling that some day soon everyone in the Southwest would know of the Tumbling Weed.

"But don't you get lonely out here by yourself?"

A muscle in his cheek twitched. "Not at all. There are ranch hands to talk to and there's always Gram."

"But what about...?" Meghan bit down on her bottom lip, holding back her intrusive question.

"You surely aren't going to ask me about my social life, are you?"

Heat blazed in her cheeks. "Sorry. None of my business. An occupational hazard."

His dark brows rose, disappearing beneath the brim of his Stetson. "Do you interview people on your show?"

"Sometimes. It's always fun to have local celebrities on as guests. I really shouldn't have pried into your private life. I was just trying to get to know you."

"If it makes you feel better, I don't have a girlfriend or anyone special. I'm not into serious relationships."

His answer put her at ease. However, the fact that his status mattered to her at all was worrisome. He was her temporary boss—nothing more. As a single expectant mother, she didn't have any right to notice a man—even if he *was* a drop-dead sexy cowboy.

Tuesday's late-morning sunshine rained down on Meghan, warming her skin and raising her spirits. She had come to anticipate her daily walks to Martha's house. It provided her with a chance to stretch her legs and inhale the sweet fresh air. At this moment her problems didn't seem insurmountable. She could...no, she *would* conquer them.

Upon reaching Martha's place, she knocked on the door. From the beginning, Martha had insisted she not stand on formalities and let herself in, so Meghan eased open the door and stepped inside, finding the house surprisingly quiet.

"Hello? Martha? I'm here to help with lunch," she said loudly, in case her dear friend hadn't heard the knock. "I also have a question for you—"

The words died on her lips when she stepped into the kitchen and found it vacant. A closer inspection revealed lunch hadn't been started, which was quite unlike Martha, who always stayed a step ahead of everyone. Meghan's stomached tightened into a hard lump.

Please don't let anything have happened to her.

A search of the remainder of the house turned up nothing. Where in the world had she gone? Martha hadn't mentioned anything at breakfast. This just didn't make sense.

On her way out the door Meghan noticed a folded piece of paper propped up on the kitchen table. Her name had been scrawled across the front. She grasped the page and started to read.

Meg,
Sorry to leave in such a rush. Amy Santiago just gave birth to triplets and is having complications. She has no family in town, so I'm going to stay with them until their

relatives arrive in a few days. Cash will
make sure you have everything you need.
See you soon.
Martha

Meghan refolded the paper and slid it in her
pocket. She couldn't help but wonder if this
would change things with Cash. Would he want
her to stay on? Or would this be the perfect excuse for him to send her packing?

CHAPTER SEVEN

"WHAT DO YOU mean, Gram's gone?"

Cash's spine straightened as every muscle in his body tensed. Why would Gram disappear without talking to him? Had it been an emergency? His chest tightened.

"You didn't know?" Meg asked, surprise written all over her delicate features.

"Of course not." He swung out of the saddle of a brown and white paint. In three long strides he reached the white rail fence where Meg waited. "Would I be asking you if I did?"

"It's just that I would have thought she'd tell you…would have asked you for a ride."

"Quit rambling and tell me where my grandmother went."

Meg yanked a piece of paper from her back pocket and held it out to him. He snatched it from her, eager to get to the bottom of this not-so-fun mystery.

His gaze eagerly scanned the page. Relief settled over him as he blew out a sigh of relief.

"Don't worry me like that again." He handed the paper back to Meg. "Gram is fiercely independent. And sometimes she gets herself into trouble."

"If you don't mind me asking, what sort of things does she do?"

"You wouldn't believe it." He shoved up his Stetson and ran a hand over his forehead. "One time I actually found her on the roof."

"The roof?" Meg's eyes rounded. "Why in the world was she up there?"

"She said it was the only way she could get the upstairs windows cleaned. There was a smudge, and she couldn't reach it from the inside. With her, I never know what's going to happen next."

A smile lifted Meg's lips, which stirred a warm sensation in him. He shoved aside the reaction, refusing to acknowledge that she held any sort of power over him.

"What did you do about your grandmother while you were away on the rodeo circuit?"

"I worried. A lot. I tried to call home every day, and I had Hal, my foreman, check in a couple of times a day."

"I can't even imagine how tough that must have been for you." She paused and her gaze lowered. "I suppose with your grandmother away you'll want me to pack my things?"

The thought hadn't crossed his mind until she'd mentioned it. Her leaving would certainly make his life a lot easier. He'd no longer have to worry about the press tracking her down. And he could relax, no longer tormented by his urge to see if she tasted as sweet as she looked.

He cleared his throat. "If you give me a chance to clean up, I can give you a lift wherever you want to go."

Her gaze didn't meet his as she shook her head. "I don't want to be a bother."

"You aren't. I'm the one who offered. Where do you want to go? Home?"

She caught her lower lip between her teeth. When she lifted her head, he saw uncertainty reflected in her green eyes. She didn't have any clue what her next move would be. Sympathy welled up in him.

No. This wasn't his problem. She'd be fine.

Or would she be?

He couldn't just kick her to the curb. If his grandmother had dismissed *him* as not her problem he'd have ended up as a street urchin at best... At worst— No, he didn't want to go there. He'd slammed the door on his past a long time ago.

Against his better judgment he heard himself say, "On second thought, if you aren't in a hurry to go I could use your help."

Surprise quickly followed by suspicion filtered across her face. "I don't need charity."

She still had her pride. Good for her.

"What I have in mind is purely business. With you here acting as housekeeper and cook I've been able to get more work done than ever before. Besides, my grandmother won't be gone long."

The stress lines eased on her face. "Are you sure?"

Absolutely not. It was crazy to invite this sexy redhead to stay here…alone…with him. But what choice did he have?

"I'm sure," he lied.

A hesitant smile spread across her face, plumping up her pale cheeks. "Since it's just the two of us, maybe we could christen your new kitchen?"

"Fine by me."

She climbed down from where she'd been perched on the fence. "Any special request for dinner?"

"Meat and potatoes are my favorite, but the fridge and pantry are almost bare. So whatever you come up with will do. I'll pick up a few things in town later today."

"I noticed there isn't any wine. Sometimes I

like to cook with it. Would you mind picking up some red and white?"

Cash clenched his jaw. He knew it wasn't her fault. She didn't know about his past, and that was for the best. If only she'd let the subject drop.

"You *do* like wine, don't you?" Her gaze probed him. "If you tell me your preference—"

"I don't drink," he said sharply.

She jumped. Regret consumed him for letting his bottled-up emotions escape. But he couldn't explain himself. He couldn't dredge up the memories he'd found so hard to push to the far recesses of his mind.

"Uh...no problem. I can cook without it."

He lowered his head and rubbed the back of his neck. "I didn't mean to startle you."

"You didn't."

She was lying, and they both knew it, but he didn't call her on it. He just wanted to pretend the incident hadn't happened.

Meg had turned to walk away when he called out, "If you'd make up a store list it'll be easier for both of us."

She glanced over her shoulder. "I'll do it first thing."

"Good."

"I'll have to remember to add a pie for dessert." She turned fully around. "You *do* like pie, don't you?"

His previous tension rolled away. "I thought the Jiffy Cook would whip one up from scratch."

"Not this girl. I can cook almost anything, but when it comes to baking I'm a disaster. Trust me, you wouldn't want to try one of my pies. Last time I tried the crust was burnt on the edges and raw in the center."

"Hard to believe someone as talented as you can't throw together a pie."

Color infused her cheeks. "My younger sister, Ella, got all the baking genes. In fact she runs her own bakery."

"If she bakes half as good as you cook, her pies must be the best in the land."

Meg's beaming smile caught his attention. His gaze latched onto her lips—her very kissable lips. His stomach dipped like it had when he was a kid riding a rollercoaster.

Damn. What had he gotten himself into by agreeing to let her stay?

A slight tremor shook Meghan's hands.

Why in the world was she letting herself get so worked up about this meal? So maybe she'd experimented a bit? That wasn't anything new. She'd been putting her twist on recipes since she was a kid.

But this was her first attempt to cook for Cash without his grandmother taking charge of the meal. Tonight's menu was spicier than anything they'd had since she'd arrived. She could barely sit still as she waited for his opinion.

"What do you think?" she asked as the forkful of flat enchilada slipped past his lips.

His eyes twinkled but he didn't answer. She watched as he slowly chewed. When his Adam's apple rose and fell as he swallowed she couldn't stand the suspense.

"Well—tell me. Did you like it?"

He rested the fork on the side of his plate, steepled his fingers together and narrowed his eyes on her. Her nails dug into her palms as she awaited his verdict. Patience had never been one of her strong suits.

Unable to stand it anymore, she blurted out, "Enough with the looks. Tell me the good, the bad or the ugly. I can take it."

She couldn't. Not really. His opinion meant more to her than a judge's at a national cooking competition. Her breath was suspended while she waited.

"So you want my real opinion, right?" he asked, poker-faced. "The unvarnished truth?"

She pulled back her shoulders and nodded.

"The enchiladas were…surprising. I wasn't expecting a fried egg inside. And the sauce was tangy, but not hot enough to drown out the Monterey Jack or the onion." He broke into a smile. "Where did you find the recipe? I'll have to try it sometime."

The pent-up air whooshed from her lungs. "Honest? I mean you aren't saying this just to be nice?"

"Me? Nice? Never."

She started to laugh. "Would you quit joking around?"

"You still didn't say where you got the recipe."

She sat up a little straighter. "That's because I didn't have a recipe. I made it up."

He grabbed her fork and held it out to her. "Then I suggest you try your own dish."

He had a good point. She'd been so wrapped up in his reaction that she'd forgotten to have a bite. How could she let this man's opinion matter so much to her? When had he become so important?

By dwelling on this current of awareness sizzling between them she was only giving it more power over her. And the last thing she or her baby needed was another complication—even if this complication came with the most delightful lips that evoked spine-tingling sensations.

She stared down at her untouched food.

Concentrate on the food—not the cowboy.

Even as a portion of the casserole rested on her plate it held its shape. Of course, she'd let it cool for about ten minutes before serving. Presentation was half the battle. No one wanted to slave away in the kitchen and have their masterpiece turn out to be a sloppy, oozing mess on the plate. And you never wanted one dish to flow into the other. That would be enough to ruin the whole meal.

So aroma and presentation passed. Now for texture and taste. A dish that turned to mush was never appetizing, nor would it be fulfilling. There had to be solidity. Kind of like Cash, who was firm and solid on the outside, but inside, on those rare insightful moments, his soft center showed.

Oh, boy, now she was comparing the man to her culinary creation. Yikes, was she in trouble?

She lifted the fork to her lips. The dish was good, but it was those riveting eyes across the table that held her captive. If only she could create a dish that made a person think they'd floated up to the heavens with each mouthful— like Cash could make her feel whenever his gaze held hers—then she'd be the most famous cook in the world.

"Something wrong with the food?" His brows creased together.

"Um…no." Heat crept into her cheeks. Thank

goodness one of his talents wasn't reading minds.

"You should be writing your own recipes."

His statement triggered a memory. "You know, it's funny that you mention it. There was this book editor once who wanted to know if I'd be interested in writing a cookbook."

"What did you tell her?"

Meghan shrugged. "That I'd think about it."

"If this is any indication of your other recipes I'd say you'd be a big hit." He helped himself to another heaping forkful of enchilada.

She couldn't hold back a grin. She did have a lot of fun creating unique food combinations. She couldn't imagine it'd be too hard to come up with enough recipes to fill a book. In fact it might be fun, now that Harold wasn't around discouraging her.

"You know, I received an email from the editor not too long ago."

"Why don't you talk to her and see what she has to offer?"

Cash was so different from Harold. Where Cash encouraged her to follow her dreams, Harold had insisted writing a cookbook would be a waste of time. She'd been so intent on pleasing him—on earning his love—that she'd gone along with his decision. She'd been willing to sacrifice her dreams to fulfill her mother's wish for her to become the perfect wife. The memory sickened her.

"I'll get back to her," Meghan said with conviction.

For a while they ate quietly. Meghan tried to focus her thoughts on anything but the sexy cowboy sitting across the table from her. Giving in to this crush would not be good. Soon she would be leaving the Tumbling Weed, and she needed to keep her focus on her baby and her options for the future.

"So what happened?" Cash asked, drawing her back to the here and now. "What made you run away from your own wedding?"

Wow! That had come out of nowhere. Her fork clanked onto her plate. She sat back and met his intense gaze. She'd suspected he'd ask sooner or later, but this evening she'd wanted it to be all about the food—the one thing she could do well. Not about her failings as a woman.

"We...we wanted different things."

His gaze continued to probe her. "You guys didn't talk about the future and what each of you wanted?"

She stared down at her still full plate. "We did. But things changed."

"And Harold wasn't up to handling change?"

What was up with all of these questions? Why the sudden curiosity? She pulled her shoulders back and lifted her chin. The determined look in his eyes said he wasn't going to let the subject rest until she'd answered him—but it didn't have to be the whole truth.

"A couple of weeks before the wedding I told him about some changes to our future and…and he seemed to accept it. It wasn't until the day of the wedding that he called everything off."

"I don't understand. If he called off the wedding why were you both at the church? Why did you walk down the aisle?" Before she could say a word, Cash's eyes widened. "Wait. You mean he waited to dump you until you were standing at the altar in front of your family and friends?"

She nodded, unable to find the courage to add that Harold had not only rejected her, but their unborn baby too. The memory of the whole awful event made her stomach churn.

"The jerk! How could he do that to you? You must have been horrified. No wonder you ran. You must hate him."

"No," she said adamantly. When Cash sent her a startled look, she added, "I can't hate him. It…it wasn't all his fault."

She'd been the one to forget her birth control pills. She'd strayed from their perfectly planned-out life. Maybe the problem was that they'd planned everything out *too* well—leaving no room for the unexpected.

"How can you stand up for him after what he did to you?"

She couldn't spout hateful things about the father of her baby—no matter how hard it was to smother the urge. "I don't want to talk about him."

"You mean you're still hung up on this guy?"

She didn't answer as she picked up her dinner plate and headed to the kitchen. Maybe she should have told Cash about the baby. Guilt gnawed at her over this lie of omission. But she couldn't see how revealing her pregnancy would change things for the better.

The last thing she wanted was for Cash to look at her as if she was an utter fool. She valued his opinion and needed him to respect her. If only she could keep her secret for a little longer he'd never have to know.

CHAPTER EIGHT

MEG'S STOMACH FLUTTERED with nerves. What had gotten into her yesterday when she'd promised Cash that she'd contact the book editor?

What if the woman had already found someone else? Or, worse, what if the editor had completely forgotten about the offer *and* her? This wasn't a good idea.

But she had promised, and she always tried to do her best to keep her word. So she sat down at Cash's computer and started it up.

Without her cell phone she felt totally disconnected from the world—cocooned in the safety of the sprawling Tumbling Weed Ranch. The thought of having to face the reality of her life and the aftermath of the wedding disaster made her heart palpitate and her palms grow moist.

Staring at the blank screen, she realized she was being melodramatic. It wasn't as if anyone was going to know she was online and confront her.

Slowly her fingertips poked at the keyboard. As was her ritual, she visited the discussion thread on the Jiffy Cook's television show website.

Any other day she'd log on to find out how people had responded to her previous broadcast. Today was different. Today her morbid curiosity demanded to know how her fans were reacting to her wedding debacle.

What would happen to her television career if her followers bailed on her? The thought of being jobless and pregnant had her worrying her lower lip. That wouldn't happen. It couldn't. Her show was doing well.

Meghan scrolled down to find over nine hundred comments. *Wow!* That was a record. Apparently people had a lot of emotions concerning her runaway bride act. Now the question remained: did the majority side with her or the groom?

She clicked on the comments and waited for them to load on the screen.

Jiffy Cook Discussion—Comment #1
Hey, Jiffy Girl, hang in there. You did what you had to do. Now stick to your guns. We're behind you. SexyLegs911

The message brought a smile to her lips. Sexy-Legs911 had been Ella's screen name for years. It was a private joke since her sister had inherited their mother's short legs. And with Ella being a baker she wasn't skinny. A point their mother stressed regularly. But that didn't keep the young guys from turning their heads when Ella strolled by. It just went to show that some men liked curves on their women—no matter what their mother said.

Meghan continued skimming over the comments until she spotted a heart-stopping link: *Fickle Cook Bails on Groom for Hotter Dish.*

The backs of her eyes stung. Part of her just wanted to shut down the computer and run away, but a more powerful urge had her clicking on the link. In seconds, a picture popped up on the screen. It was from a distance, but it showed her as she'd run out the church doors.

Meghan's face flamed with heat and she blinked repeatedly as she read the malicious article. They accused her of running out on Harold for a hottie from her stage crew.

It was libelous! Outlandish! Horrible!

But it also had thousands of hits. Her shoulders slumped. By now even her own mother must think she was a two-timer with no conscience.

An internet search of her name brought up another trashy article. It included a picture of someone claiming to be her, and with the picture being slightly out of focus observers just might believe it really was. Her look-alike was on some beach, making out with a tanned, muscular guy that she'd never laid eyes on before in her life. And this headline was even more outrageous: *Jiffy Cook Dishes up New Dessert on Solo Honeymoon.*

What in the world was her family thinking after reading that scandalous trash? Her once stellar reputation was beyond tarnished—singed beyond repair. What was she to do now?

Cash was in the middle of exercising Emperor when he spotted Meg walking down the lane. He was about to turn away, but there was a rigidness in her posture—an unnatural intensity in her movements—that didn't sit right with him.

Something was wrong—*way* wrong.

"Hey, Hal!" he called out to his ranch foreman. "Can you finish up with Emperor? I need to take care of something."

Hal cast a glance in Meg's direction. "And if you don't hurry, at the pace she's moving, you'll need the pickup to catch up to her."

Cash didn't waste time responding. He swung out of the saddle and ran, vaulting over the fence. All the while he searched his memory to recall if he'd done something wrong. He couldn't think of anything. In fact she'd seemed to be in a good mood at lunch, having created a delicious frittata recipe.

"Racing off to any place in particular?" he asked, taking long strides to keep pace with her short, quick steps.

"Like you'd care," she said in a shaky voice.

Cash grabbed her arm, bringing her to a stop. "Whoa, now. What has you so riled up? And, by the way, I do care. Now, out with it."

She glanced up at him with red-rimmed eyes. The pitiful look tugged at him, filling him with a strong urge to pull her to his chest and hold her. But her crossed arms and jutted-out chin told him the effort would be wasted.

"I'm waiting," he said. "And we aren't moving until I know what's going on."

A moment of strained silence passed. "You'll think it's stupid."

"I doubt that."

"Why?"

"Because you don't strike me as the type to get this upset over something trivial."

Surprise closely followed by relief was reflected in her bloodshot eyes. "I went online to contact the book editor and…"

"She turned you down that fast?"

Meg shook her head. "There were these articles online…about me. They were…awful. Full of lies."

Her shoulders drooped as she swiped at her eyes. He inwardly groaned at his own stupidity. If he hadn't urged her to contact the editor she wouldn't have run across the bad press.

He had to make this better for her. Throwing caution to the wind, he reached out and wrapped his hands around her waist. Surprisingly, she came to him without a fight. Her cheek pressed to his chest.

His heart hammered as he ran a hand over her silky hair. She felt so right there. So good.

"I'm sorry," he murmured.

She yanked out of his hold. "Why should you be sorry? You didn't write those malicious lies."

He lifted his hat and raked his fingers through his hair. "No, but I've been on the receiving end of the tabloid press. I know how bad it can hurt."

She eyed him. "Is that why you hide away here—all alone?"

"I'm not hiding." Or was he? It didn't matter. This wasn't about him. "Don't try and turn the tables on me."

"Just seems, with you being a good-looking guy and all, you wouldn't have a hard time finding someone to settle down with."

His heart thumped into his ribs. She thought he was good-looking?

Now wasn't the time to explore what that might mean. Right now she was upset and trying her hardest to change the subject. But he couldn't let the press stop her from having the brilliant future she so deserved.

"Meg, this isn't about me and my decisions. You have to ignore the lies. Because the more you say about the matter, the more headlines you'll make for them. And you don't want them to make a bigger deal of this, do you?"

A fire lit in her eyes. "Of course not."

"Good. Anyone who knows you will know it's nothing but a pack of lies. Give it a little time and they'll move on to the next story."

The stress lines eased on her face, which in turn eased the tightness in his chest. He wanted to go online and call those people out on their lies—he wanted to tell the whole world that Meg was the kindest person he'd ever met. She'd no more intentionally hurt someone than he would return to the grueling life of the rodeo circuit.

He fought back the urge. He couldn't make this any worse for her. All he could do was be there for her when she needed a friend.

Not liking the thought of her returning to a career where the press took potshots at her, he asked, "Did you contact the book editor?"

Meg shook her head, letting the sunshine glisten off the golden highlights in her red hair. "I was going to, but then I saw those awful articles—"

"Don't dwell on them. They aren't worth it. Pretend they don't exist and go ahead with your plan to email the editor."

"But if my reputation is already smeared in the press, what's the point?"

He *hated* that some lowlife had made Meg doubt herself. "Trust me, those articles aren't such a big deal."

Her gaze narrowed. "Really? Or are you trying to make me feel better?"

"I'm serious." And he was. He doubted anyone would give those headlines any credence. "Now, promise me you'll contact the editor."

A wave of expressions washed across her pale face. Seconds later her shoulders drew back, her chin tilted up and her gaze met his. "I'll do it."

Late the next afternoon, Cash stared down at the large check made out to the Tumbling Weed and couldn't help but smile. Emperor's new owner had just picked up the black stallion. The sale couldn't have come at a better time. The ranch could certainly use a few more profitable sales like this one.

He couldn't wait to share the good news with Meg. His strides were long and fast as he made his way to the house. Inside, he found some pans on the stove, but no sign of his beautiful cook.

"Hey, Meg?" Nearly bursting with pride over

his biggest sale to date, he searched downstairs for her.

"I'm in the family room."

In his stockinged feet, he moved quietly over the hardwood floors. Meg turned as he entered the room. Her smile was bright like the summer sun. It filled him with a warmth that started on the inside and worked its way out. He tamped down the unfamiliar response. He couldn't let himself get carried away.

"You never told me you were a world champion steer wrestler." A note of awe carried in her voice as she held up a trophy. "I'm not sure this room is big enough to display all of your accomplishments. Shame on you for hiding all of these awards in a box in the corner."

His chest puffed up a little. "You really like them?"

"I think they're amazing—*you're* amazing. And very brave."

Brave? No one had ever used that word to describe him. He could tell her some horror stories from his days on the rodeo circuit, but he didn't want to ruin this moment. He felt a connection to her—something so strong he wasn't sure he'd ever experienced it before.

"I was lucky," he said. "I retired before anything too serious happened to me."

"I'm glad." She picked up another trophy. "Any particular place you want these?"

"Wherever you think is best works for me."

She immediately turned and began positioning the two awards on the mantel. "What did you come rushing in here to tell me?"

Oh, that's right. He'd gotten so caught up in Meg and her compliments that he'd forgotten his big news. "The buyer just picked up Emperor. I've made my first big sale. And the man promised to be back for more."

"That's wonderful! Congratulations. I've got some good news too."

"Are you going to make me guess?"

She grinned like a little kid with a big secret. "I followed your advice and found the email from that book editor. I reread it. She sounded very excited about the project. I can only hope she's still interested. I emailed her and now I'm waiting to hear back."

Cash basked in Meg's happy glow. He'd never seen anyone look so excited and hopeful. With all of his being he willed this to work out for her.

"The editor's going to jump on this opportunity."

"We need to celebrate," she said. "And I just happen to have your favorite meal started in the kitchen. I'd better go check on it."

She remembered his favorite meal? He paused

and looked at her. He couldn't deny it. He was impressed. She was a diligent worker—in fact his house had never been so clean, with a fresh lemony scent lingering in the air—she'd befriended his grandmother in record time, and she was thoughtful.

He liked this—he liked *her*. There was so much more to Meg than he'd originally thought possible for a television celebrity. She wasn't at all concerned about herself, but she cared for others.

He trailed behind her into the kitchen. His gaze latched onto her finely rounded backside as she sashayed across the room. His blood warmed at the sight, bringing his body to full attention.

His gaze slid down over her shorts to her bare legs. He stifled a murmur of approval. Still, he couldn't stop his mind from imagining what it would be like to run his hands over her creamy smooth skin.

She turned to him and heat flamed from beneath his shirt collar, singeing his face. His mouth grew dry and he struggled to swallow.

He should turn away, but he couldn't. He liked staring at her too much. Every day he swore she grew more beautiful. She was like a blooming flower. Even the dark circles under her eyes had faded since she'd been here. He'd also taken note of her increased appetite. For the second time the blue skies and fresh air of the Tumbling Weed had worked its magic and healed a broken person—he'd been the first, when he'd returned here a few months back.

Meg rushed around the kitchen. "Do you see the hot mitts?"

He spotted them on the counter and moved into action. "Let me get the food from the oven."

"I've got it." She snagged the mitts from his hand, moved to the oven and removed the aluminum foil from a casserole dish. "Not yet. The roast needs a few more minutes."

"Sure smells good," he said, making small talk since his grandmother wasn't around to fill in the silent gaps.

"Thanks." She adjusted the oven and reset the timer. "I hope you like it."

"If it tastes half as good as I think it will, you don't have a thing to worry about."

She grabbed a serving spoon from the ceramic canister on the counter and turned to him. Her smile sparked a desire in him that raced through his body like wildfire, obliterating his best intentions.

The tip of her pink tongue swiped over her full bottom lip. "I experimented with it. You might be taking your life in your hands by trying it."

"Where's the fun if you don't take a risk now and then?" His gaze never wavered from her mouth. "Have I thanked you properly for all you've done?"

"No, you haven't." Her eyes grew round and sparkled with devilry. "What did you have in mind?"

He stepped up to her and wrapped his hands around her waist. Any lingering common sense went up in smoke. With a slight tug, she swayed against him. Her hands splayed across his chest. Could she feel the pounding of his heart? Was hers pounding just as hard?

Her voluptuous curves pressed against him and all he could think about was kissing her… holding her…having her. His gaze met hers. The want…the need…it was written in her smoldering eyes. Was this the way she'd stared at Harold?

Cash froze. His chest tightened. The thought hit him like a bucket of icy water. The last thing he wanted to think about was old what's-his-name. And he certainly didn't want to think about him or anyone else kissing Meg.

The brush of her fingertip along his jaw reheated his blood. Dismissing the unwanted thoughts, he gazed back at Meg. Before he could make his move she stood up on her tiptoes and leaned into him. Was this truly happening? Was she going to kiss him? Or had he let his day-dreams run amok?

Her breath tickled his neck and her citrusy scent wrapped around him. This was certainly no dream. And if by chance it was he didn't want it to end. Meg fit perfectly in his arms, like she'd been made for him.

With her pressed flush against him he was helpless to hide his most primal response to her. Her mouth hovered within an inch of his, but she stopped. Had she changed her mind?

When she didn't pull away he dipped his head. His lips brushed tentatively across hers. He longed for a deeper, more intense sampling, but he couldn't rush her. This moment had to be right for both of them. He'd never wanted someone so much.

A slight whimper met his ears. He hoped it'd come from her, but at this point he couldn't be sure. He took the fact she was still in his arms as an invitation. Their lips pressed together once again and there was no doubt in her kiss. She wanted him too. His hold on her waist tightened until no air existed between their bodies.

She tasted sweet like sun-warmed tea. He didn't want to stop drinking in her sugary good-ness. Their kiss grew in intensity. His fingers worked their way beneath her top. Her skin was heated and satiny smooth. He wanted to explore every inch of her. Here. Now.

He'd never met anyone like Meg—a woman who could drive him to distraction with a mere look or the hypnotic sway of her luscious curves. Yet in the next moment she could make him want to pull his hair out with her fierce determinedness.

Now, as her hips ground into his, he wanted nothing more than to shed the thin layer of clothing separating them and make love to her right there in the kitchen. What would she say? Dared he try?

His fingers slid up her sides until his fingertips brushed over her lacy bra. He'd slipped his hands around to her back, anxious to find the hook, when an intrusive beeping sound halted his delicious plan.

"The food!" Meg pushed him away and rushed over to the oven. "I can't let it burn."

If anything was burning it was him. His body was on fire for her and his chance of being put out of his misery had slipped right through his fingers.

He strode across the room, stopping by the window—as far as he could get from Meg without walking out on her. His clenched hands pressed down on the windowsill. His gaze zeroed in on the acres of green pasture. But it was the memory of Meg's ravaged lips and the unbridled passion in her eyes that held his attention. He raked his fingers through his hair. What was he doing? He hadn't been thinking. He'd merely acted on impulse.

As he cooled off he realized that for the first time in his life he'd let his desires overrule his common sense. Meg had teased him with those short-shorts and tempting lips, and he'd forgotten that she was a runaway bride, hiding out here while she pieced her life back together. The mere thought of how he'd lost control shook him to the core.

Thankfully they'd been literally saved by the bell. Otherwise she still might be in his arms, and things most certainly would have moved beyond first base. He expelled a long, frustrated sigh. He'd really screwed up. How in the world were they supposed to forget that soul-searing kiss and act like housemates now?

CHAPTER NINE

MEGHAN FLOPPED ABOUT her bed most of the night. She couldn't wipe that stirring kiss from her memory, but it was Cash's reaction—or rather his lack of a reaction—since then that ate at her. Life had merely returned to the status quo.

She rose long before the sun and hustled through her morning routine. With her energy back and her stomach settled, Meghan couldn't stand the thought of spending another day cooped up in the house. Besides, Cash made her job easy since he had a habit of picking up after himself. She appreciated the fact he didn't take advantage of her being the housekeeper. He was such a gentleman.

He'd certainly make some woman a fine husband—if only they could lasso him. A frown pulled at her lips. The thought of another woman in his arms left her quite unsettled.

Still, with his stirring kisses it was only a

matter of time before someone took him permanently off the market. She'd certainly never experienced such passion in a kiss before. Not even close. So what was different? What was it about Cash that made her insides do gymnastics? Or was it simply that the grass was greener on the other side of the fence?

She tried to recall her first dates with Harold. They were hazy and hard to remember. Not a stellar commentary on the man she'd almost married and the father of her unborn baby.

The harder she thought about it, the more certain she was that Harold had never once excited her with just a look. He'd never watched her with such rapt interest. They had simply started as good friends with parallel goals. Somewhere along the way they'd gotten caught in a dream of being the perfect power couple.

But, even though Cash's kiss had touched her in a way no other kiss ever had, she had to put it out of her mind. With no firm plans in place to return to her life, she needed to make sure things were all right between her and the sexy cowboy.

The allure of the stables and the horses called to her. Heck, she could work a shovel and wheelbarrow with the best of them. She'd used to help her mother every spring by turning the soil in the vegetable garden—a garden which had expanded each year. How different could it be cleaning up after horses? What she didn't know, she'd learn.

Dressed in blue jeans and the borrowed boots, she trudged to the barn, ready for work. She glanced around the corral but didn't spot Cash. The doors were open on the stables, as they had been since she'd arrived here. Shadows danced in the building as a gentle breeze carried with it the combination of horses, hay and wood. The rustic scents reminded her of a certain cowboy and a smile pulled at her lips.

Cash stepped out of a stall leading a golden-brown mare. He stopped in his tracks. "Did you need something?"

"Point out what needs to be done out here and I'll get started."

"You mean you want to shovel horse manure?" When she nodded, he lifted his tan cowboy hat and scratched his forehead. "Don't you have enough to do inside?"

She crossed her arms and didn't budge. "I need a change of pace."

"Wait here," he said. "I'm taking Brown Sugar outside."

"No problem. Growing up, I spent a lot of time at my best friend's ranch. I loved it and wished I'd grown up on one." She shrugged. "Anyway, I still remember a thing or two."

Cash walked away, leaving her alone except for the few other horses still lingering in their stalls. The place was peaceful. She understood why Cash loved this ranch. Perhaps if the cookbook deal worked out and she made some extra money she could buy a small plot of land for herself and the baby. The thought filled her with hope.

Meghan strolled down the wide aisle, peering into the empty stalls. At the far end she made her way over to one of the occupied stalls. An engraved wooden plaque on the door read "Nutmeg." The mare stuck her head out the opening and Meg ran her hand down over the sleek neck.

"Hey, girl. Ready to stretch your legs?"

The horse, as though understanding her, lifted her chin.

"Have you made a new friend?"

The sound of Cash's voice caused Meghan to jump.

She whirled around to face him. "You startled me."

He held up both hands in defense. "Sorry. But you've got to pay more attention to your surroundings if you intend to spend time around the horses."

"Where would you like me to start?"

He eyed her up. "You're really serious about this?"

She nodded.

"Do you think you're up to walking Nutmeg out to the corral?"

"Definitely. We were just becoming friends."

When he stepped closer to help with the horse the quivering in her stomach kicked up a notch. No man had a right to be so good-looking. If he smiled more often he'd have every available female in New Mexico swooning at his feet. And she'd be the first in line.

Meghan got to work. She wasn't here to drool over him. She wanted to earn her keep and prove to him that they could still get along.

Cash watched as she led the mare outside. Meg's curly ponytail swished from side to side. He couldn't turn away. He drank in the vision of her like a thirsty man lost in the desert. There were no two ways about it: he was crazy to agree to work with this beautiful redhead who could heat his blood with the gentle sway of her hips.

He should have turned her away, but when her green eyes had pleaded with him he'd folded faster than a house of cards in a windstorm. He sighed. No point in beating himself up over his weakness when it came to Meg. Besides, maybe it'd do her some good, having a chance to live out her childhood dream of living on a ranch. He wondered how real life would compare. Probably not very well.

When he'd first arrived at the Tumbling Weed he'd believed all his problems were in the past. Not even close. As a child, he hadn't had the capacity to realize his father had most likely got his mean streak from Cash's grandfather.

Cash had started for the tackroom when the sound of an approaching vehicle had him changing directions. He couldn't think who it would be—perhaps a potential buyer? His steps came a little faster. Slowly but surely the reputation of Tumbling Weed had been getting out into the horse community, drawing in new customers.

He stepped out of the stable and a flash went off in his face. He blinked, regaining his vision only to find a stranger with a camera in his hand. A growl rose in the back of Cash's throat. He didn't need anyone to tell him that this smug-looking trespasser was a reporter.

"Aren't you Cash Sullivan, the two-time world steer-wrestling champion?" The man, who appeared to be about his own age, approached him with his hand extended.

Cash's shoulders grew rigid. His neck muscles tightened. He'd bet the whole ranch this reporter wasn't here to do an article on his horse-breeding business. He crossed his arms and the man's hand lowered. "What do you want?"

"A man who gets straight to the point. Good. Let's get down to business—"

"You can start by explaining why you're on my ranch."

The man's brows rose. "So you're admitting you're Cash Sullivan? The man who started a life of crime at an early age? What was it?" He snapped his fingers. "Got it. You held up a liquor store with your old man."

The muscles in Cash's clenched jaw throbbed. This reporter had certainly done his homework and he wasn't afraid to turn up the heat. Cash refused to defend himself. No matter what he said it'd be twisted and used against him in the papers.

When silence ensued, the reporter added, "And weren't you a suspect in the rodeo robbery earlier this year?"

Cash lowered his arms with his hands fisted. Every bit of willpower went into holding back his desire to take a swing at this jerk. A little voice in the back of his mind reminded him that an assault charge certainly wouldn't help his already colorful background.

With all his buttons pushed, Cash spoke up. "Funny how you forgot to add the part where I was never charged with either crime. If you guys don't have a good story you conjure one up. Now, get off my property."

The man didn't budge. "Not until you tell me if you've stolen another man's bride."

Cash glared at the man. Did this fool have a clue how close he was to being physically removed from the Tumbling Weed?

"How do you know her? Have you two been lovers all along?"

Cash flexed his fists and stepped forward. "For your own safety, leave. Now."

The man's eyes widened but he didn't retreat. "So my question struck a chord? Where are you hiding the runaway bride?"

The man peered around. Cash wanted to glance over his shoulder to make sure Meg hadn't followed him out of the barn, but he couldn't afford to give anything away. There was no way he'd let this man get anywhere near her.

"I don't know what you're talking about. There's no woman around here."

"You don't remember being at that church at the time of the bride's mysterious escape?"

Cash's gaze narrowed in on the man. This was the reporter who'd asked him if he'd seen which way Meg had gone. How much did he know?

"Why bother me? Shouldn't you be checking out her home? Or speaking with her family?"

What had led this man to his doorstep? Were

there more reporters behind him? A sickening sensation churned in his gut.

The reporter rubbed his stubbled jaw. "The thing is she hasn't been home and her family doesn't have a clue where she is. Seems you're the last person to see her. I'm thinking she tossed over the groom for her lover. I'll just have a look around and ask her myself."

Cash's open hand thumped against the guy's chest, sending him stumbling back toward his car. "You're trespassing. If you take one more step on my ranch you'll be facing the sheriff."

The man narrowed his gaze on him, as though trying to figure out if he was serious. Cash put on his best poker face, meeting the man's intense stare dead-on. At last all those late nights of card playing out on the rodeo circuit had paid off.

"What if my publisher was willing to make this worth your while?"

"I don't have anything to tell you. You're sniffing 'round the wrong cowboy and the wrong ranch. You've been warned."

The man yanked a card out of his pocket. "If you change your mind, call me. Don't take too long. If the rumors and public interest die so does my offer."

When Cash didn't make a move to accept the card, the man reached out and boldly stuffed it in Cash's shirt pocket. Finally the man turned and climbed back in his car. Cash didn't move until the vehicle had disappeared from sight.

He pulled the card out and ripped it up. This wasn't over. As sure as he was standing there on this red earth the rumors would begin to swell. His past would be dug up—again.

No matter what he did, he'd never escape his past. In the end he would only end up damaging Meg's reputation even more. If he'd ever needed a reminder of why he was better off alone this was it.

He'd never be a good boyfriend, much less husband material.

This fact stabbed at his chest deeply and repeatedly.

Cash turned and headed for the barn. At least Meg had had the presence of mind to stay hidden while the reporter had been snooping around.

"Meg, you can come out now."

He detected a whimper. His eyes took a moment to adjust to the dim lighting after being in the bright sunshine.

"Help me…" Meg's voice wavered.

He scanned the area and saw her lying on her side. His heart galloped faster than his finest quarter horse. He rushed to her side and crouched down.

"Did you break something?" Her watery eyes stared up at him. He wished she'd say something—anything. "Meg, you've got to tell me what's wrong."

"I was running to hide from the reporter and…and I slipped." Her bottom lip quivered.

He reached out and tucked a loose strand of hair behind her ear before letting his hand slide down to caress her soft cheek. "Do you think you can get up?"

"I…I think so. But what if I hurt the baby?"

The baby? A shaft of fear sliced into him. He snatched his hand back from her. She sure didn't look pregnant.

"How…how far along are you?"

"Not very. But I can't lose it." A silent tear splashed onto her pale cheek.

"I'll call an ambulance." He reached for his cell phone.

"No—wait."

"You're in pain. You should go get checked out right away."

"Help me up." She held out a hand to him.

"You sure that's a good idea?"

"Never mind." Exasperation threaded through her weak voice. "I'll do it on my own."

Figuring he couldn't make things any worse than having her struggle to get up on her own, he moved swiftly and slipped his hands under her arms. She was a solid girl, but he easily helped her to her feet. His hands lingered around her as he studied her face for signs of distress.

"Any pain?" If she said yes he didn't care how much she protested. He was throwing her in his truck and rushing her to the emergency room.

She shook her head.

"You're sure?"

She nodded.

He wished she'd talk more. It wasn't like her to be so quiet. "Let's get you inside."

Guilt and concern swamped his mind, making his head throb. This whole accident was his fault. He should have kept a closer eye on her. He'd never forgive himself if something happened to her or her baby.

A baby. Meg was pregnant. The fragmented thoughts pelted him, leaving him stunned. What was he supposed to do now?

Once the shock wore off Meghan breathed easier. Thank goodness there was no pain or cramping. Before she could take a step toward the ranch house Cash swung her up in his arms.

"What are you doing? Put me down."

He ignored her protests as he started for the house at a brisk pace. Her hands automatically wrapped around his neck. A solid column of muscle lay beneath her fingertips. A whiff of soap mingled with a spicy scent teased her nose.

She wanted to relax and rest her head against his shoulder, but she couldn't let herself get caught up in the moment. Cash had so many walls erected around his heart that she doubted a wrecking ball could break through. With all her own problems she didn't need to toy around with the idea of getting involved with someone who was emotionally off-limits.

He carried her into the family room and approached the leather couch. Meghan glanced down. A manure smudge trailed up her leg. "Don't put me down here. I'm filthy."

"It'll clean up."

"Cash, no."

Ignoring her protest, he deposited her with the utmost care onto the couch. The man could be so infuriating, but she wasn't up for an argument. Once she'd rested for a bit, assured herself everything was all right with the baby, she'd grab the leather cleaner and spiff everything up. After all, it was her job.

"Can I get you anything?" he asked, breaking into her thoughts.

"No, thanks. I'm okay now."

He sat down on the large wooden coffee table and leaned forward, resting his elbows on his knees. "No aches or pains? The baby—?"

"Is fine." When Cash made no move to leave, she added, "You don't need to sit there the rest of the day, staring at me."

He leaned back and rubbed the stubble lining his jaw. "You have to tell me the honest truth. Do you need a doctor?"

She reached out and patted his leg, noticing the firm muscles beneath his denim. "Other than needing another shower, I feel fine. If things change you'll be the first I tell."

"Promise?"

Her hand moved protectively to her abdomen. "I've got a little one to protect now. I'll do whatever it takes to give him or her the best life."

"Does that include sticking by the father even if he doesn't deserve your loyalty?"

CHAPTER TEN

MEGHAN STUDIED CASH'S face, wondering what had given him the idea she was in any way standing by Harold. After the thoughtless, hurtful manner in which he'd dumped her, nothing could be further from the truth.

"Why in the world would you think I feel loyalty toward Harold?"

Cash's dark brow arched. "I don't know. How about because you wanted to save your wedding dress? You wore your engagement ring until you started doing housework, and you refuse to say a bad word about him."

Oh, she had a whole host of not-so-nice things to say about Harold, but she refused to give in to the temptation—it'd be too easy. And she didn't want her child exposed to an atmosphere where animosity was the *status quo*.

However, Cash had opened his home to her, and he hadn't needed to. And once he'd gotten to know her he'd been kind and generous. It was time she trusted him. He deserved to know the unvarnished truth.

She inhaled a steadying breath and launched into the events leading up to her mad dash out of the church, including how Harold had rejected not only her but also their baby.

Cash's eyes opened wide with surprise. "He doesn't want his own baby?"

She shook her head.

Cash's expression hardened and his eyes narrowed. "How can he write off his own kid as if it was a houseplant he didn't want? Doesn't he realize how lucky he is? I'd give anything to have my baby…"

The impact of his words took a few seconds to sink in. Dumbfounded, she stared at him. Lingering pain was reflected in his darkened eyes.

At last finding her voice, she asked, "You're a father?"

His head lowered. "I never got the chance to be. My ex didn't want to be tied down."

Meghan squeezed his hand. His fingers closed around hers and held on tight.

"I'm so sorry," she said. "But maybe some-day—"

"No. It's better this way." He released his hold on her and took a step back. "Are you sure you want to be a mother?"

Meghan nodded vigorously. "Besides, even if I had done what Harold wanted he still wouldn't have married me. It just wasn't meant to be."

"So there's no chance of a reconciliation?" Cash's direct gaze searched her face.

"Absolutely none." Instead of pain and regret, all she felt was relief.

"I guess this is the part where I'm supposed to say I'm sorry it didn't work out, but it sounds like you were lucky to find out the truth before you married him."

Meghan sighed. "My mother wouldn't agree with you. She had this perfect wedding planned. In fact, she expected me to be the perfect wife to the perfect husband and live out the perfect life."

"That's a tall order, considering nothing and no one is perfect."

"Try explaining that to my mother. She likes to run with the 'in' crowd and pretend our family is better than we are. No matter how hard I've tried I've never earned her approval. But when I started dating Harold she became a little less critical of me and she smiled a little more."

"I'm guessing she isn't happy about the wedding being called off."

Sadness over not being able to turn to her own mother during this trying time settled over her. "Once again I've disappointed her. And she doesn't even know that I'm about to become a single parent."

"Doesn't sound like your mother is going to be much help with the baby. What will you do?"

"For the time being I'm going to keep my pregnancy under wraps and go back to my job as the Jiffy Cook."

"I thought you didn't like the job? Why not try something else?"

"I can't. I'm pregnant. I no longer have the freedom to pick and choose what I do for a living. I have to do what is best for my child."

Cash's brow arched. "And you think being the Jiffy Cook is the best option?"

"It provides a comfortable income and excellent health benefits."

"But if you aren't happy—"

"I don't have a choice."

"What about Harold? He's still the baby's father."

The thought of her child growing up without a father deeply troubled her. Both of her parents had played significant roles in her life. Her mother had given her the gift of cooking, for which she'd be forever grateful, and her father had taught her to keep putting one foot in front of the other, day after day, no matter the challenges that lay ahead. How in the world would she ever be enough for her child?

"For the baby's sake I'll make peace with Harold. We'll work out visitation. Or, if he really wants nothing to do with the baby, I'll have him sign over his rights."

Cash nodded in understanding. "Sounds like you've been doing a lot of thinking since you've been here. You know there's still the press to deal with? Seems they're more fascinated with you than I first thought."

The memory of why she'd slipped and fallen came rushing back to her. "What did you tell the reporter when he was here?"

"Nothing." Stress lines marred his face. "The reporter was the same man I spoke to at the church when we were leaving. I don't think he knows anything definite, but I can't promise he won't be back."

She noted how his lips pressed together in a firm line. In his gray eyes she spied unease.

"What else is bothering you?"

The silence engulfed them. She wouldn't back down. She had to know what was eating at him.

Cash got to his feet and paced. He raked his fingers through his hair, scattering the short strands into an unruly mess. He stopped in front of her, resting his hands on his waist.

His intense gaze caught and held hers. "Fine. You want to know what keeps going through my mind?" She nodded and he continued. "You didn't tell me you were pregnant."

He was right. She'd been lying by omission. And none of the excuses she'd been feeding herself now seemed acceptable. She'd never thought about it from his perspective. "I…I'm sorry. The timing just never seemed right. I shouldn't have let it stop me. I should have worked up the courage to be honest with you—"

All of a sudden there was a movement in her abdomen. Her hands moved to her midsection.

Cash rushed to her side and dropped to his knees. "Is it the baby? Are you in pain?"

She smiled and shook her head. It was the first time she'd ever felt anything like it.

"Meg, talk to me or I'm calling an ambulance."

Pulling herself together, she said, "I swear I'm not in pain."

"Then what is it?"

She grabbed his hand and pressed it to her tiny baby bump. "There it is again."

He pressed both strong hands to her stomach. His brows drew together as though he were in deep concentration. "I don't feel anything. Was the baby kicking?"

"When I found out I was pregnant I started to read a baby book. At nine weeks the baby's too small to kick, but there was a definite fluttering sensation."

"Sounds like you have a feisty one in there." His expression grew serious. "Promise me you'll be more cautious from now on? That little one is counting on you."

She blinked back a sudden rush of tears and nodded. She wasn't a crier. It must be the crazy pregnancy hormones that had her all choked up.

When Cash moved away a coldness settled in where his hands had been pressed against her. She didn't want him to go. Not yet. But she didn't have a reason for him to stay.

"Don't move from that couch until I return." He bent over and snatched his cowboy hat from the coffee table. As he stood, his gaze met hers. "I won't be gone long. I have to speak with Hal and let him know if he needs me I'll be right here, taking care of you."

His orders struck her the wrong way. "No."

"Meg, don't be ridiculous. You need to rest. And I'll be here to make sure that you do just that."

The idea of listening to him sounded so good—so tempting. But the fact she wanted to let him take charge frightened her. She couldn't need him—want him. The last time she'd leaned on a man he'd taken over her life. This time she needed to make her way on her own.

She swallowed hard. "I can take care of myself."

"Quit being stubborn."

"Just leave me alone," she said, struggling to keep her warring emotions in check. "I don't need you. I don't need anyone. I can take care of myself and my baby."

Cash expelled an exasperated sigh but didn't say another word.

His retreating footsteps echoed through the room. Once the front door snicked shut a hot tear splashed onto her cheek. She dashed it away with the back of her hand, but it was quickly followed by another one. These darn pregnancy hormones had her acting all out of sorts.

She refused to accept that her emotional breakdown had anything to do with her wishing Cash was her baby's daddy, not Harold. Because if she accepted that then she'd have to accept she had feelings for him. And she didn't have any room in her life for a man.

Cash stomped out to the barn, tossed his hat on the bench in the tackroom and raked his hair with his fingers. His thoughts kept circling over the conversation he'd had with Meg. He was trying to figure out where it'd run off the tracks. One minute he was offering to help her and the next she was yelling at him.

No matter how long he lived, he'd never understand women. They'd be mankind's last unsolved mystery. He kicked at a clump of dirt, sending it skidding out into the aisle.

What was he supposed to do now? The thought of Meg packing her bags and leaving played on his mind. Worry inched up his spine. He hoped she wouldn't do anything so foolish.

He was thankful for one thing—Gram wasn't here to witness how he'd screwed things up. If Meg left early because of him…because he'd overstepped the mark…his grandmother wouldn't forgive him—he wouldn't forgive himself.

His cell phone buzzed. He didn't feel like talking to anyone, but with a ranch to run he didn't have the luxury of ignoring potentially important calls. "Tumbling Weed Ranch."

"Cash, is that you?" Gram shouted into the phone as though she were having a hard time hearing him.

"Yep, it's me. Ready to come home?" Talk about lousy timing. What he didn't need at this moment was a lecture about how he'd blown things with Meg.

"I'm not ready to leave yet. Amy's mother had problems catching a flight, but she's supposed to be here by next week. I agreed to stay until then. How are things there?"

Talk about a loaded question. He couldn't tell Gram about Meg—not over the phone. Besides, Gram already had her hands full caring for a new mother and her babies. She didn't need to hear about *his* problems.

"Cash?" Gram called out. "Cash, are you still there?"

"I'm here. Things are going well. Not only has Meg finished cleaning your house, but she almost has mine spiffed up too."

"You aren't working that poor girl too hard, are you? She needs to take care of herself and get plenty of rest."

Gram *knew* Meg was pregnant. The knowledge stole his breath. Why had he only just learned about it? A slow burn started in his gut. He'd been the last to know when his mother and father had run out of money. And the last to know when his dad had planned to hold up a liquor store.

Then, earlier this year, he'd been the last to know when his girlfriend, who'd worked in the office at the rodeo, had been in cahoots with a parolee. Behind his back they'd ripped off the rodeo proceeds and framed him for the job. She'd claimed he owed her. Instead of giving her his prize money, to fritter away at the local saloon, he'd always sent it home to Gram for the upkeep of the ranch. Thank goodness he'd had an alibi.

And now this. Meg had confided in his grandmother about her condition but she hadn't seen fit to share it with him, even though he'd opened his home up to her. His hand tightened on the phone.

"When did she tell you?" he asked.

"Tell me about what?" Gram asked a little too innocently.

"Don't pretend you don't know she's pregnant. You've known all along."

A slight pause ensued. "It wasn't my place to tell you."

"What else have I been kept in the dark about?"

"Nothing. And why does it bother you so much? It's not like you're the father."

Gram paused, giving him time to think. He might not be the biological father but he already had a sense of responsibility to this baby and its mother. His jaw tightened. He knew it'd lead to nothing but trouble.

"Cash, you're not planning to get involved with Meghan, are you?"

"What?" He would have thought his grandmother would be thrilled with the idea of him settling down with Meg, not warning him against it. "Of course not."

"Good. I know you've had a rough life, and

trusting people doesn't come easily to you. That girl has been through enough already, and with a baby on the way she doesn't need another heartbreak. She needs someone steady. Someone she can rely on."

His grandmother's warning shook him. He wanted to disagree with her. But she was right. This wasn't his baby.

"Don't worry," he said. "Nothing's going to happen. Soon she'll be gone."

"I didn't say to run the poor girl off. She has a lot to deal with before she returns home. I have to go. One of the babies is crying. Tell Meghan I've come across some unique recipes while I've been here. We can try them out when I get home."

Without a chance for him to utter a goodbye the line went dead. Gram was expecting Meg to be here when she returned. If Gram found her gone she'd blame *him*. He'd already caused his grandmother enough heartache for one lifetime. He didn't want to be responsible for Meg leaving without Gram having an opportunity to say good-bye.

CHAPTER ELEVEN

THE WARM GLOW of the afternoon sun filled Cash's bedroom. Meghan swiped a dust rag over a silver picture frame with a snapshot of a little boy cuddled in a woman's arms. She pulled the picture closer and studied the child's face. The familiar gray eyes combined with the crop of dark hair resembled Cash. She smiled back at the picture of the grinning little boy. Was the beautiful woman gazing so lovingly at the child his mother? Meghan wondered what had happened to her. And where was Cash's father?

So many unanswered questions. She shoved away her curiosity. None of this was any of her business. She ran the rag over the frame one last time before placing it back on the dresser.

His bedroom was the last room to be cleaned. She gave the place a final inspection, closed the windows and dropped the blinds. Sadness welled up in her as she pulled the door shut behind her. With both houses clean she needed to make plans to leave—especially after her total meltdown the day before.

Even so, she'd come to love this house and ranch so much in such a short amount of time. She'd been able to relax here and be herself. If only she could get her life back on track—back to normal. Whatever *that* was. Then she'd be just as comfortable back in Albuquerque as she was here. Wouldn't she?

After putting away the cleaning supplies and grabbing a quick shower she realized it was five o'clock and she still hadn't started dinner. With exhaustion settling in, she decided to go with an easy meal. Spaghetti marinara with a tossed salad.

While the sauce simmered, Meghan took a moment to check if there'd been a response from the book editor. This time she made a point of avoiding any blogs or articles about herself. Her empty stomach quivered in anticipation as her fingers clicked over the keyboard.

She opened her email account, finding a bunch of new messages. The third one down caught her attention. It was from Lillian Henry, the editor. Meg's heart skipped a beat before her nerves kicked up a notch. Was Lillian still interested? Or had the bad press swayed her decision? Questions and doubts whirled through

Meghan's mind as her finger hovered over the open button.

Taking a deep breath, she clicked on Lillian's name and the email flashed up on the screen.

To: JiffyCook@myemail.com
From: Lillian.Henry@emailservice.com
RE: Cookbook
Hello, Meghan. I was surprised to get your email, considering everything that's been happening in your life. I'm happy to hear you're interested. Let me know when you're available to discuss a theme for the book series. I'm looking forward to some sample recipes. Lillian

Meghan jumped to her feet and did a happy dance around the kitchen island, laughing and squealing in delight. *A series. Wow!* Things were looking up for her at last. She couldn't stop smiling.

She'd need to rethink how to fit in enough time to work up additional recipes and figure out themes for these books. There was so much to plan—but then again, planning things was her forte. Now, with a baby to care for, a demanding television show and books to write, she'd definitely need a new strategy to make time for everything.

She started for the door to tell Cash, but as

her hand touched the doorknob she paused. Since she'd told him to leave her alone, he'd done just that. Other than a couple of inquiries about her well-being and the baby's, no words had passed between them.

Meghan's excitement ebbed away.

With no one to talk to, Meghan returned to the computer. She scrolled down through the list of unrecognizable names until she came across one from her producer at the TV studio.

To: JiffyCook@myemail.com
From: Darlene.Jansen@myemail.com
RE: Urgent!
Meghan, where are you? What happened? We need to talk right away. Call me. Darlene Jansen

Guilt washed over Meghan. She'd been MIA longer than was appropriate, but her time at the Tumbling Weed had been so nice—so stress-free. Now it was all about to end.

She grabbed the phone and dialed her producer. On the second ring she picked up.

"Where have you been?" Darlene asked, cutting straight to the chase. "Do you know what has been going on around here? The suits upstairs were real unhappy when the television special about your wedding fell through. All the buildup and the money we spent on advertisements to pique viewer interest and we ended up having to air a rerun. Ratings plummeted."

A baseball-sized lump swelled at the back of Meghan's throat. She swallowed hard and it thudded into her stomach. Television was a ratings game. Up until this point her ratings had been impressive—so impressive they'd been working on moving the Jiffy Cook to a larger audience.

"I'm sorry, Darlene." Now wasn't the time to remind her producer that she had been opposed to promoting the wedding week after week. They'd covered everything from floral arrangements to choosing the right wedding dress. It'd just been too much.

"Couldn't you have gone through with the ceremony?" Darlene asked. "If you really didn't want to be married, you could have had it annulled later."

Meghan's mouth gaped. Was she *serious?* Sure, she might have been planning to marry Harold out of obligation to their child, but that was different than saying "I do" to impress the public while planning an annulment the next morning.

Trying to smooth the waters, Meghan said, "Listen, I'll be back in town tomorrow. How about we get together for lunch and discuss how you want to handle things for the next show?"

Ignoring the lunch invitation, Darlene plowed on. "Why did you walk out on the ceremony when you knew it was being taped to air on the next show?"

With her job on the line, Meghan decided it was time she came clean and let the broken pieces of her life fall as they may. Surely Darlene would sympathize with her after she'd heard the details.

"I'd just found out I'm...I'm pregnant."

A swift intake of air filled the phone line, followed by an ominous silence. Not at all the reaction Meghan had been expecting. Darlene had always been friendly and supportive before. She obviously didn't know her as well as she'd thought.

Too late to turn back, so Meghan ventured forth. "Harold waited until we were at the altar to tell me he didn't want...the baby." She exhaled an uneven breath. "He didn't want me. I...I couldn't think about anything but getting away from him...from the church."

A tense silence ensued. Unsure what else she could say in her own defense, Meghan quietly waited.

"This won't help us," Darlene said in a firm tone. "After you ran out on your wedding, the execs got the impression you're fickle. They're not going to pick up the show on a national basis."

"But they don't know the circumstances. The wedding was personal, not business."

"None of that matters to them. They believe you're spoiled and selfish. That you'll balk at the first rough spot."

Meghan's body tensed. "Who gave them that impression?"

"Doesn't matter."

She didn't need confirmation. Her gut said it had been Harold. He could be a wonderful ally, but if he thought someone had crossed him he wouldn't rest until he'd leveled his enemy. Apparently he truly believed she'd intentionally gotten pregnant and he'd done her out of her job. How could he be so vindictive?

She paced back and forth, needing to keep her rising temper in check while she approached this conversation from a different direction. "But I've been working toward this point in my career since I took my first waitress job when I was sixteen. I've always worked in the food industry."

"Your work history is a long list of pitstops before you moved on to the next rung on the ladder. It doesn't display any stability."

Meghan's hand spread over her abdomen. "There has to be a way to renew my show in its former spot. Surely they'll understand. I can bring the numbers back up."

"Your old time slot has been filled. You knew it was going to be a gamble when we put the show out there to be picked up on a larger platform."

Meghan's mouth gaped and she sucked in a horrified gasp. She remembered the meetings about moving the Jiffy Cook from her half-hour spot for a small audience around Albuquerque to an hour-long broadcast for a national audience. She'd met with Darlene and the executives. And then she'd discussed it with Harold. Everyone had been in agreement that with the rising ratings the sky was the limit. Now the sky was raining down all over Meghan, and there wasn't an umbrella big enough to protect her.

"You've been great to work with," Darlene said in weary voice, "and I thought you had a bright future ahead of you. But the suits want what they were promised—a career-oriented woman. Now, with the ratings at an all-time low, I have to tell the execs that your priorities will soon be split between your career and being a single mom."

Meghan blinked away the sting at the back of her eyes. "I can manage a career and a family."

"They don't care. All they care about is the bottom line. That's why I've been trying to reach you. Word came down on Monday to shut down the show."

A sob caught in the back of her throat as her eyes burned with unshed tears. This couldn't be happening. Her life kept spinning out of control and she didn't know how to stop it.

Cash strode up to the house late that evening. He'd put off talking to Meg as long as possible. But a sandwich and chips just didn't go far when you were spending the afternoon breaking in a horse. And not even the most stubborn stallion could erase his thoughts of Meg. In fact at one point he'd lost his hold when the horse had bucked and nearly landed on his injured shoulder. Another slip like that and he'd be back in the hospital—a place he hoped never to see again.

A part of him knew he'd let himself begin to care about Meg more than he should, but this silent treatment was a bit of overkill. Maybe he should apologize…but for what?

His temples began to throb. He didn't know what he'd done wrong. Could he have overreacted when he found out about the baby? That had to be it. He'd apologize and they'd make peace.

He hoped.

Cash quietly let himself into the mudroom at

the back of the house. His motions were slow after his rugged workout. His shoulder ached from the repeated abuse. He rubbed the tender area with his other hand.

He pulled off his dirty boots and set them aside. In his stockinged feet, his footsteps were silent as he crossed to the entrance to the kitchen. He spotted Meg with her back to him. The soft glow of the stove light illuminated her curves. His immediate reaction was to go to her and wrap his arms around her before nuzzling her neck. But he held himself to the spot on the hardwood floor. He didn't need to muddy the waters by sending her mixed signals.

Cash took a closer look and noticed the way her head was bent and her shoulders slumped. Had she been lying when she'd told him she was okay after the fall? Was something wrong with the baby? Or maybe this was just one of those pregnancy hormone fluctuations?

A sniffle caught his full attention. His chest tightened. If there was something wrong with her or the baby and he'd left her alone all day he'd never forgive himself.

He strode over to her. "Are you okay?"

Her spine straightened, but she kept her back to him. "I'm fine. Your dinner is ready."

He placed his hand on her shoulder. "I'm not

interested in the food. It's you I'm concerned about. Turn around and talk to me."

She didn't budge. "Go wash up."

Alarm sliced through him. *Please don't let anything be wrong with the baby.*

The child might not have his DNA but he felt a connection to it. He knew what it was like to be rejected by your biological father. No child should ever go through that pain.

The fact the baby was part of Meg had him conjuring up an image of a little girl. Cute as a button with red curls and green eyes just like her mother. But soon Meg was leaving, and he'd never get the chance to know the baby.

"Meg, you aren't listening to me. I don't want dinner. I want you to face me and tell me what's wrong."

"Nothing. Just leave it alone." The pitch of her voice was too high.

"I'm not moving until you start giving me some answers."

Not about to continue talking to her back, he tightened his hand on her shoulder as he pivoted her around to face him. Her eyes were bloodshot and her cheeks tearstained. He didn't take time to consider his next action. He merely reached out and pulled her into his embrace.

Her lush curves pressed against his hard length. He was surprised when she willingly leaned into him. Her arms draped around his midsection while her head drooped against his chest. She fit so perfectly against him—as though she'd been made for him.

Her emotions bubbled over and he let her cry it out of her system. He pressed his lips to her hair and breathed in her intoxicating scent. His hand moved to the length of red curls trailing down her back. For so long he'd ached to run his fingers through the silky mass and at last he caved in to his desire. Nothing should feel so soft or smell so good. He took a deep breath, inhaling the faint floral scent. It teased his senses, making him want more of this woman.

His body grew tense as he resisted the urge to turn this intimate moment into something much more—a chance to caress her body and chase away those unsettling tears. He knew it was wrong—she was pregnant, and a local celebrity, totally out of this broken-down cowboy's league. But that didn't douse his longing to protect and comfort her. Nor did it diminish the mounting need to love away her worries.

When her tears stopped, he mustered up all his self-restraint and moved so that he was holding her at arm's length—a much safer distance. What she needed now was a friend, not a lover. If only his libido would listen to his mind.

"Meg, if it's not the baby, what has you so upset? Let me help you."

She shook her head. "You can't."

CHAPTER TWELVE

CASH REFUSED TO give up. Meg needed him, and he intended to find a way to make things better for her. "If this is about me overreacting about the baby, I'm sorry."

She pulled back to look up at him. "It doesn't have anything to do with that."

Her eyes shimmered with unshed tears and her face was blotchy. Her pouty lips beckoned to him. If only a kiss could make her worries disappear he'd be more than willing to ride to her rescue. He gave himself a mental jerk. A kiss would only complicate matters.

"Will dinner be okay for a little bit?" he asked, wanting to get her off her feet.

She nodded. "I turned the burners off."

"Come with me." He led her to the family room, where they sat side by side on the couch. "Now, tell me what has you so worked up."

When a fresh tear splashed onto her cheek, his body tensed. Not sure what to do, he grabbed a handful of tissues from the end table and stuffed them in her hand. His gaze strayed from her to the door. He stifled the urge to make a beeline back to the stables. Out there, he knew what to do. In here, he didn't have the foggiest idea if he should hold her again or sit by patiently until she stopped sniffling and started talking.

"Did someone die?" he asked, needing to know the severity of the situation.

She hiccupped and shook her head. "It's nothing like that. I think the pregnancy hormones have me overreacting."

He let out a pent-up breath and squeezed her hand. "It's okay. You just worried me."

Long seconds passed as Meg dashed away tears with a tissue and blew her red nose. "I heard back from the book editor."

Oh, no, had the editor changed her mind? The woman had to be crazy, because Meg made the most delicious dishes. He should know—his waistline was increasing from the second and third helpings he had regularly at each dinner.

"What did she say?" he asked, already searching for words of support.

"She wants to get together and discuss the idea of writing a series of cookbooks."

Confused, he said, "Sounds like good news to me."

"You think so?"

"Of course I do. Otherwise I wouldn't have encouraged you to contact her."

"That's one of the things I like about you—your straightforward answers."

One of the things she liked about him implied there were more. A warm sensation filled his chest and made his heart pound. He wanted to know what other things she liked, but resisted the urge to ask.

He was having trouble figuring out her problem, but he didn't want to say too much and get the waterworks flowing again. He was certain if he waited she'd tell him more. Women liked to talk about what bothered them—wasn't that what his grandmother had told him?

Meg balled up the tissue in her hand. "While I was checking my email I came across one from my television producer." The color drained from her cheeks. "She needed to talk to me so I called her. She…she told me the deal to move my show to a bigger platform had fallen through."

Ah—now he understood. "I'm sorry." His sympathy did nothing to ease the pain etched on her face. He should say something else—something to calm her worries and give her hope. "Maybe if your show keeps doing well they'll make the change next year?"

She shook her head. "You don't understand… there's no show. *The Jiffy Cook* has been cancelled. I was worried this might happen if we went ahead with plans to move to a larger platform, but Darlene assured me with the ratings the show was generating it'd be a sure thing. And I believed her. I thought she was my friend. I thought wrong. I've been so wrong about so many people in my life."

Cash sat back on the couch, resisting the urge to pull her back in his arms and kiss her until she forgot her problems. He didn't want to end up being another person who let her down. And leading her on when they had nowhere to go would certainly qualify.

"What am I going to do?" She threw herself back against the couch and hugged her arms over her chest. "I need those health benefits."

Secretly, he thought this was for the best. Meg could find a better job—a more stable one. A job that would make her happy.

He glanced over at her. The light had gone out in her eyes. It knocked him for a loop. Meg was a gutsy woman. Someone he'd come to admire for her spunk and determination. Until now, he'd never seen her utterly give up—not even after the father of her baby dumped her at the altar. This reaction had to be some sort of shock. She'd snap out of it. He just might have to give her a nudge.

"Don't let this defeat you," he said with conviction. "You can make new plans. Let me help you."

Her chin lifted. "I have to do this on my own."

"But why? I've got friends and they've got friends. Surely someone needs a fabulous chef?"

She shook her head. "I let myself rely on Harold and look where that got me. This time I have to do it my way."

Was she comparing *him* to Harold? The thought stung. He was nothing like that self-righteous, pompous jerk. He wanted to call her out on her comment, but the wounded look in her eyes subdued his indignation. This was about Meg, not his wounded ego.

"There's still the plan to work with the book editor," Cash offered.

Meg's green eyes opened wide and at last a little light twinkled in them. "That's true. And she didn't seem to be fazed by the wedding falling through. She said she's looking forward to receiving sample recipes."

"Sounds promising."

"I just can't believe she wants to do a whole series. How in the world will I come up with so many new dishes?"

As quickly as the light in her eyes flicked on, it dimmed again. Meg leaned back on the couch. Her emotions were bouncing up and down more than a bucking bronco. He raked his fingers through his hair. Pregnancy hormones should be outlawed. He didn't know what reaction to expect from her.

"How about we grab some food?" he asked, anxious for a distraction. "I always think more clearly on a full stomach."

"I *am* hungry." Meg rose to her feet. Her shoulders drooped, as though every problem in the world was weighing on them. "I'll set the table."

He grabbed her hand. Her fingers were cold—most likely from nerves. His thumb stroked her smooth skin as he guided her down next to him. Just a mere touch quickened his pulse. He pulled his hand away.

"You've done more than enough today. You stay here and put up your feet." He picked up the remote for the large screen television and held it out to her. "Find us a good show to watch."

He was at the doorway when Meg called out, "Cash, thank you."

"No problem. After all, you cooked it."

"Not for dinner. For listening to me and not judging me for losing my job." She got to her feet and moved until she stood directly in front of him. Her emerald eyes held a sadness which tugged at his heart. "I feel safe here with you—like I could tell you anything and you'd understand."

Her words touched a spot deep inside him. He swallowed hard, feeling a thump-thump in his chest. It was a place he'd thought had all but died, but Meg had shown him that his heart might be damaged but it could still feel the intensity of her words. Maybe somewhere, somehow, with Meg around, there was a spark of hope for him.

"We'll get through this together." He pulled her into his arms and held her close, drawing on her strength to bolster his own. "I won't let you down."

"I know you won't."

Her faith in him made him want to move the sun and the stars for her. But what was he doing, making promises to a pregnant woman? Especially promises he didn't know if he could keep—if he *should* keep.

Meghan's bare feet were propped up on the coffee table, exactly where Cash had placed her after the comforting hug. How had she gotten so lucky to have someone so caring in her life?

She flipped through the various television stations. She wasn't used to a man waiting on her. Her father had been old-fashioned and had expected to find dinner on the table. Then there had been Harold, and he'd liked to be waited on as though he were royalty. At first she hadn't minded. She'd thought he'd eventually do the same for her. But he had never returned the gesture. And she'd begun to wonder if all men expected to be catered to.

Cash had renewed her belief that there were still gentlemen in this world. She hoped when the right lady came along and landed him she would realize what a wonderful man she'd married. The thought of another woman sitting here, waiting to share a cozy meal with him, brought a frown to Meghan's face. She was being silly. It wasn't like she had any claim on him. They were friends. Period.

"Here you go." Cash held a big plate of spaghetti in one hand and the salad in the other. "I'll be right back with your drink."

When he handed over the food their fingers touched. Awareness pulsed up her arm and settled into a warm spot in her chest. As he returned to the kitchen she found herself turning to appreciate his finer assets. How had this man managed to stay single all these years?

The fact he didn't mind treating her like a princess only added to his irresistibility. In that moment she knew the man she married would have to have this quality. Thoughtfulness went a long way in her book. But, sadly, this sexy cowboy no more fit into her city life than she could be a world-famous cook on an out-of-the-way ranch.

At last they settled side by side on the couch with their feet up. Meghan worked the remote, scanning the television stations. When they stumbled over a crime series she paused and turned a pleading look to Cash. "Do you like this?"

"It's fine by me."

She grinned. "I love this show. But you have to guess the killer."

"I do?"

She nodded, excited to have someone to share her favorite television show with at last. "It's no fun otherwise."

He glanced over at her with an arched brow. "And what if—?"

"Shh…it's on. We'll miss the clues."

He chuckled as he settled back against the couch. She couldn't remember the last time she'd been home to catch an episode. It seemed as though the past year of her life had been one long string of dinners out on the town or mandatory appearances at various events.

An hour later the empty dishes were piled at the end of the coffee table because neither wanted to risk missing any of the show. Each threw out guesses about the villain's identity, and at the end Cash got it right.

"Since you guessed the killer, I'll clean up," Meghan said, getting to her feet.

"I don't think so." He picked up the stack of dishes and started for the kitchen. "You cooked. I'll take care of the rest."

This man was offering to clean up? Had she died and gone to heaven? Even if all he did was rinse them off and stack them in the dishwasher she'd be tickled pink.

She followed him. "Are you serious?"

"Would you quit acting so shocked?" He sat his load on the counter and turned to her. "It isn't that big a deal."

"If you're sure." He nodded and she added, "I should give my sister a call."

He momentarily frowned. "Is this sister the one you called right after the wedding?"

"Yes. Ella is a couple of years younger than me. We used to be really close."

"Maybe with the baby on its way it'll draw you two back together."

She smiled at Cash's encouraging words. He reminded her of her father and his peacemaking tendencies. "I hope so. I'm pretty sure my mother will want nothing to do with me or the baby after the way I screwed up the wedding."

Disappointment and frustration welled up in her as she faced the fact that she'd come so close to receiving her mother's approval at last, only to have it snatched away. She promised herself never to be so hard on her own child.

"I take it your sister won't be so judgmental?" he asked.

"I don't think so. You should meet her sometime. I think you'd like her." She regretted the words as soon as she spoke them.

He smiled and the dimple in his cheek showed. "I'd like that."

His comment implied they had a future, but she knew that wouldn't be the case. Once she left the Tumbling Weed she'd never be back. She'd mail him a check for all the clothes and then this part of her life would be done—over— a memory.

Sorrow settled in her chest. So many doors were being closed to her. She needed to start throwing open some windows until she found a way out of this mess.

CHAPTER THIRTEEN

CASH YAWNED AS he strolled to the kitchen early the next morning and flicked on the ceiling light. He wanted to help Meg, but she'd told him point-blank not to. It just wasn't in his nature to stand by and not lend a hand. What would it take to get that stubborn redhead to see reason?

He moved to the cabinet where he usually kept the coffee grounds but found none. Funny... he'd just picked some up at the store. They must be around somewhere. A quick search revealed they were on the bottom shelf of the fridge. He smiled. Little changes had been made all over the house but he didn't mind a bit. It was nice to share the place with someone.

"Morning." A long yawn followed Meg's greeting. "I slept in."

He turned, ready to shoo her back to bed, but when his gaze landed on her cute pink cotton top and sleeper shorts, all rational thoughts fled his mind. His gaze lingered on her skimpy outfit, which revealed her smooth, bare legs. His blood stirred. With each heartbeat his temperature shot up another degree.

Realizing he was staring, he jerked his line of vision upward. Another yawn overtook her and she stretched. The tiny T-shirt rode up, giving him a glimpse of her creamy midriff. He shifted uncomfortably, fighting the urge to go to her.

"Sorry I'm still in my PJs. When I saw the time I rushed down here. I didn't want you to skip breakfast."

"You should go back to bed." He forced himself to turn away from the tempting view. He breathed in a deep, calming breath before he proceeded to add grounds to the coffeemaker. "I've got everything under control."

With the machine armed with coffee and water, he switched it on. Having regained his composure, he turned to find her heading for the refrigerator.

"Stop," he said. "You aren't cooking this morning."

She paused. The overhead light made her squint as she turned to him, but it was the return of the dark shadows beneath her eyes that concerned him.

"Of course I am."

"Did you get any sleep last night?"

She shrugged. "After I talked to my sister I had trouble falling asleep."

And he knew exactly what had kept her awake—the loss of her job. His hands clenched and his jaw tightened. He could help alleviate some of her worries if she'd just let him.

Unable to keep his mouth shut, he said, "I'll make some calls today and see if I can track down some leads for you."

Her shoulders squared and her hands balled and rested on her hips. "We talked about this, I don't need charity. If I'm going to be a mom I've got to learn to do things on my own."

"But it's just a little help—"

"No. Thank you."

He'd certainly give her credit for fierce determination to gain her independence. And, as much as he wanted to argue with her, the pursing of her lush lips and the slant of her eyes told him he needed to find another tactic.

All this stress couldn't be good for her or the baby. If she wouldn't let him help her find a job, he could at least help distract her from her problems for a little bit.

"You know, you've been working too hard around here," he said. "When we made our agreement I never meant for you to clean the house top to bottom."

"But I wanted to do it. You didn't have to

open your house up to me but you did. And I'm extremely grateful."

"And I'm glad I was there to help. But I don't want you to overdo it. Especially with the baby and all…"

Pink tinged her cheeks. "I am a little tired."

"Then go crawl back in bed."

"But what about breakfast—?"

"I can grab something to eat. I'm not helpless." Not giving her time to protest, he added, "If you do as I ask I've got an offer for you. How would you feel about packing us a picnic lunch?"

"A picnic?" Her face lit up.

"I'll saddle up a couple of horses and we'll take off about eleven. What do you say?"

"I say it's a date." Another yawn had her covering her mouth. "It's been years since I was on a picnic. I can't wait."

She sauntered out of the kitchen. His gaze followed the pendulum movement of her hips until she turned the corner. He expelled a sigh of regret.

Soon she'd be gone and, boy, was he going to miss everything about her. No one but his grandmother had ever gone out of their way for him. His house not only sparkled, but bit by bit she'd made it into a home. Somehow he would find a way to pay her back.

* * *

Meghan sat atop Cinnamon, trying not to frown. In between preparing food for the picnic she'd searched the online job notices. She hadn't found any openings for a chef, but she refused to let it defeat her.

She'd taken the time to update her résumé and sent it out to a number of restaurants in Albuquerque. It was only after she'd hit "send" that the nerves had settled in. What if none of them called her? What would she do next?

She'd deal with that later.

Right now, with the sun's rays warming her back and the handsomest cowboy on her left, she made a concerted effort to shove her problems to the back of her mind. It wasn't every day such a sexy guy asked her out on a picnic.

With a gentle breeze at their backs, they quietly rode along with no particular destination in mind. Out here it was just them, their horses and an abundance of nature. Meghan inhaled deeply, enjoying the fresh air laced with the scent of grass and wildflowers.

Cash was easy to be around. He talked when he had something to say, but never just to hear himself talk. And he listened to her—really listened. He made her feel special. She only wished she could make him feel the same way.

He worked so hard, from dawn until late in

the evening, never once complaining, but instead insisting on helping her with the dinner dishes. That was why she'd worked extra hard on this picnic lunch. He deserved a special treat.

After riding for an hour or so they came upon a winding creek. Off to the side was a lush green pasture, just perfect for a secluded picnic—a romantic rendezvous. Was it possible Cash had more in mind for today's outing than just food? She cast him a sideways glance. He wasn't acting any different than normal.

"Can we stop here?" she asked.

Her overactive imagination conjured up an image of her spreading out a blanket and sinking down into Cash's arms. His gaze would catch hers, stealing her breath away. And before she knew it his lips would be pressed to hers. The daydream sparked heat in her cheeks.

The level of her desire for him struck her. She'd never hungered for a man in her life. She worried at her bottom lip. She was carrying one man's baby and craving the touch of another. Did this make her some sort of hussy?

"Why are you frowning?" His voice cut into her troubled thoughts. "Did you change your mind about stopping?"

"No, this is fine. In fact it's beautiful. You're so lucky to own this little bit of heaven on earth."

"Really? Because you looked like something was bothering you."

"Nothing." She forced a smile. "Although I'm getting hungry. How about you?"

"Definitely. The aroma of fried chicken has been pure torture."

She was being silly and worrying for no reason. But when he helped her out of her saddle she noticed how his hands lingered a little longer than necessary. His gaze caught hers and his Adam's apple bobbed.

In the next breath he pulled away. "I'll grab the food."

In no time Cash set the supplies down at her feet. They included a container of homemade potato salad, macaroni and cheese and some deviled eggs. "If you don't need anything else, I'm going to take the horses down to the creek."

"Go ahead. I'll be fine here. Lunch will be ready when you get back."

"I won't be gone long." His gaze paused on her lips, causing her insides to flutter. "Promise you won't start without me?"

She swallowed and tried to maintain an easy demeanor. "Now, would I do something like that?"

He strolled over to the horses. Wise or foolish, she couldn't ignore the magnetic attraction pulling at them. Cash felt it too. She was certain of it.

And it wasn't just now that he'd felt it. This morning in the kitchen she'd caught his hungry glances. And there had been other times when he'd eyed her up, all the while thinking she hadn't noticed.

She licked her dry lips. She'd most definitely noticed.

No more than ten minutes later Cash had tended to the horses and was heading back to join Meg. The aroma of fried chicken floating along in the gentle breeze was tempting, but not as tempting as having a taste of Meg's sweet kisses. This picnic was his best idea so far. And Meg looked more delicious than the cherry pie she'd packed for dessert.

When he entered the clearing she flashed him a smile. His chest puffed up. No one had ever looked at him quite that way before.

She got to her feet and moved to meet him partway. Her beauty mesmerized him, from the pink tingeing her cheeks to the spark of mischief in her emerald eyes.

"Thanks for bringing me here," she said, stopping in front of him. "I didn't think it was possible, but I'm feeling much better."

"That's great. I thought a change of scenery might help."

Her palms rested on his chest. Could she feel how her mere touch made his heart beat out of control? He hoped not. The last thing either of them needed was to let this physical attraction get out of hand.

"It's not the scenery," she said, her voice growing soft with a sexy lilt. "It's you."

Before he could make sense of what was happening she leaned closer. He couldn't let this happen—no matter how much he wanted it. He turned his head and her lips pressed against his cheek.

Meg jumped back. Her face flamed red. His gut knotted with unease. He knew that he was responsible for her embarrassment and was unsure where this would leave them.

"I thought you…um…don't you like me?" she stammered.

He lowered his head, realizing he'd been too obvious with his interest in her. "You're wonderful. It's not you, it's me."

"Seriously? You're going to throw that tired old cliché at me?" She stepped forward and raised her chin so they were making direct eye contact. "You like me. You're just afraid to admit it."

"Drop it." He tried to walk away but she grabbed his arm.

"Admit it. Admit that you can't forget about that kiss we shared back at the house. Admit that you want to do it again."

She was right. He did like her. And he thought about that stirring kiss far too often for his own sanity. Heck, he'd offer up his prize stallion to taste her lips once more—but he couldn't—they couldn't.

"Meg, stop it! This—you and me—it can't happen."

He pulled away from her touch. He had to convince her that he wasn't good enough for her. She could do so much better.

He strode over to the picnic area.

A blue-and-white quilt was spread over the ground with the food in the center. He stopped next to the blanket, unable to tear his gaze from the familiar hand-sewn material. His throat tightened and the air became trapped in his lungs.

"Why can't we happen?" Meg persisted.

He knelt down on the edge of the quilt. His outstretched fingers traced over the interlocking blocks of material. This was a physical reminder of why he had to stop this romance with Meg before it got started.

"You don't know me," he said.

Her intense stare drilled into him. "Then tell me. I'm listening."

He didn't want to have this talk—not with her—not with anyone. But he'd already said too much, and now he might as well fill her in. Maybe then she'd understand why they could never share more than a few kisses—no matter how much he longed for more.

"This quilt is older than me. My great-grandmother made it for my mother. It kept me warm in the winter, but most of all it kept me safe from the war between my parents. When I was hidden beneath it I pretended no one could see me."

He paused, wondering how many people described their parents' relationship as a war. He sure hoped not many. No child should ever live through what he'd endured. No one should ever feel the need to become invisible to stay safe.

Meg opened her mouth, obviously to offer some unwanted sympathy, but when he turned a hard gaze to her she pressed her lips back together and knelt down beside him. He'd never get it all out if she showered him with compassion. He needed to say this once and for all. Revealing his past was necessary. It'd set both of them free from this magnetic attraction.

His muscles tensed and his stomach churned as he reached into the far recesses of his mind, pulling forth the memories he'd tried for years to forget. "My mother wasn't a bad person. But she was young when she became pregnant. She wasn't ready for a husband and a child. And my father…well, he was a piece of work."

"Your mother must have been a brave woman. I'm scared to death about bringing a child into this world."

"You don't need to be afraid. You'll make a wonderful mother."

Her eyes lit up with hope. "You really think so?"

He nodded. He envisioned Meg with a baby in her arms—a baby with red hair and green eyes just like her. Sadness welled up in his chest when he realized he'd never witness mother and child together. Once she left the Tumbling Weed there'd be no looking back for either of them—it had to be that way.

"Tell me some more about your mother," she said, with genuine interest in her voice.

"She was the most beautiful woman I'd ever seen. I remember her singing me to sleep. She sang like an angel."

Meg's hand moved to her stomach. "I hope my son or daughter will have such wonderful memories of me."

Cash shook his head. "It wasn't all good. She tried to be a good mother, but she couldn't stand up to my father. He blamed her for his washed-up rodeo career. Heck, he blamed her for everything that went wrong. I'll never understand why she didn't just leave him. When the money ran out she sold our possessions—anything that would buy us food for just one more day."

"I can't imagine not knowing where your next meal was going to come from," Meg said softly. "So this is why you treat the people in your life like the horses you sell. By holding them at arm's length they can't hurt you."

"You don't understand." His hands clenched. "There's more to it. Some people shouldn't be allowed to reproduce, and my father was one of them."

Cash threw his hat down on the blanket and stabbed his fingers through his hair. Memories bombarded him. He chanced a glance at Meg. Her features had softened and her eyes were warm with…was that *love?*

His heart skipped a beat. No, it couldn't be. It had to be compassion. If it was love, they were in far more trouble than he'd ever imagined. He had no choice now but to get the rest of his past out in the open.

"When there was nothing left for my mother to sell or barter, my father's answer wasn't to get a job. Not him. Instead he loaded the family up in the car and we headed into town. We pulled up to a liquor store and he made me get out…"

Cash drew in an unsteady breath, refusing to meet Meg's unwavering stare. What was she thinking? It didn't matter. Nothing she'd imagined could come close to the horror of his dreadful tale.

"I didn't want to go. I was a frightened nine-year-old who wanted to stay in the car with my mother. My father grabbed me by my collar and yanked me out of the backseat." Cash rubbed his hand over the back of his neck, still able to recall the burn where his shirt had been pulled taut across his skin. "He dragged me to the liquor store door, pulled it open and pushed me inside. I knew by the fierce look on his face that it was going to be bad. I had no idea how bad. I was shaking when he shoved a handgun at me."

Meg expelled a horrified gasp. "What on earth was he *thinking?*"

"Probably about how to get his next drink." Cash spat out the bitter words. "When I didn't take it, he forced it into my hands. I think he said if anyone tried to come in the door I was to shoot them. I'm not real sure. I'd started crying by then."

Meg reached out to him, but he jerked back before her fingers touched his.

He gave her a hard stare, which stopped her

hand in midair. "You wanted to know why I'm damaged goods, so I'm telling you."

"I don't care what you say. You're a good person."

He ignored her protest while he dredged up the courage to finish telling her this nightmare. "I stood in the liquor store, crying and shaking. The gun dangled from my fingertips. My father yelled at the salesclerk and the next thing I heard was a gunshot. I ran out of the store and kept running until my mother pulled me into the car."

Meg placed a hand on his jean-clad thigh and this time he didn't move it. He needed her strength to get through the next part—the part that had haunted his dreams for years.

"I can't imagine how scared you must have been." Meg's soft voice was like balm on his raw scars.

"My father had left the car running, so when he ran out of the store and jumped in he punched the gas pedal. He ranted about what a wimp I was and I believed him. If I had been stronger I would have stayed by his side. I climbed into the backseat to get away from him. I knew all too well what the back of his hand felt like. In no time there were sirens behind us but my parents continued to fight. I hunched down on the floor to keep out of his reach. He started chugging stolen whiskey. That stuff always made him meaner. When he couldn't grab me, he smacked my mother. The car jerked and my mother screamed. The next thing I knew the car was wrapped around a tree and both of my parents were dead."

"That's the saddest story I've ever heard." Pity echoed in her voice, making him feel worse. "Nobody should ever have to put up with a bully like him."

"It wasn't until I was a teenager, after being around my grandfather, that I realized the apple hadn't fallen far from the tree. Both of them were tough men to get along with under the best of circumstances, but put some liquor in front of them and they became mean."

"So that explains it," Meg said.

"Explains what?"

"The reason there's no liquor in your house or Martha's. And why you reacted so negatively to my suggestion of picking up some wine in town."

"When he had the money Dad always started his evenings with a cheap bottle of wine at dinner. From there he'd move to the stronger stuff."

"I'm sorry. I should have figured there was a reason both houses are completely dry. I just wasn't thinking."

This time it was Cash who reached out and

squeezed her hand. "There was no way for you to know. But now that you do you have to understand, with a father like mine, why I'm better off keeping to myself."

CHAPTER FOURTEEN

WATER SPLASHED ONTO the back of Meghan's hand. Had it begun to rain? She glanced up at the clear blue sky. There wasn't a cloud in sight. Then she lifted a hand to her cheek, finding it damp.

She didn't know when during that sad story she'd begun to cry, but it didn't matter. All that mattered now was Cash.

She sat there in the meadow, wanting nothing more than to ease his pain. She stared across at him, noticing how the color had drained from his complexion.

What did you say to someone who'd lived through such an abusive childhood? *I'm sorry* seemed too generic—too empty. She wanted him to know how much she cared about what had happened to him. Still, words of comfort remained elusive.

She got to her knees and leaned forward. Unwilling to let the firm set of his jaw or his mask of indifference deter her, she wrapped her arms around him. With a squeeze, she wished she could absorb his pain.

"Cash, you can't beat yourself up for something that happened when you were a kid. You were a victim…not an accomplice."

He unwound her arms from his neck. "You don't understand. The bad stuff—it's in my genes."

"I don't believe it. You're nothing like your father or grandfather. But if you let the past rule your future it won't matter. You'll miss out on all of the good bits—"

"I've got to check on the horses." Cash jumped to his feet.

"Wait. Don't go." Her heart ached for him. She once more held out her hand, hoping this time he'd grab on. He had to know he wasn't alone. "I'm here for you."

Inner turmoil filtered across his tanned face. He glanced at her hand. She willed him to take it. Instead he turned and, like a wooden soldier, marched away without so much as a backward glance.

She lowered her hand to her lap. This trip down memory lane hadn't brought them closer together. In fact she'd wager their talk had only succeeded in confirming Cash's belief that he should remain a lone cowboy. The thought left a sad void inside her.

His story was so much worse than she could have ever imagined. The fact he'd lived through such horrific events and still turned out to be a caring, generous soul amazed her. But it explained why he distanced himself from everyone in his life. He was afraid of being hurt again.

Her heart clenched. She knew all too well what *that* felt like.

Giant chocolate chip cookies.

That was Meghan's answer to Cash's stony indifference. Since he'd revealed that intimate part of his life yesterday he'd locked her out. Other than a nod here or a glib answer there, they hadn't really interacted.

At dinnertime the back door clattered shut a few minutes before six. Meghan tossed a clean kitchen towel over the large platter of still warm cookies. Then she placed a homemade Mexican pizza smothered in Monterey Jack and cheddar in the oven.

With the timer set, she dusted off her hands and turned. "Dinner's just about ready."

His gaze didn't meet hers. "There's no rush."

"I made something special for dessert." She held her breath, hoping it'd pique his interest.

"That's nice." He headed out of the room, most likely on his way to get cleaned up.

The air rushed out of her lungs. Not a smile, not a glimmer of interest in his eyes or even some basic curiosity. So much for getting to a man's heart through his stomach. Obviously the person who'd made up the saying had never encountered anyone as stubborn as Cash.

She pressed her fingers to her lips, holding back a litany of frustration. She'd had it with him. If only she hadn't made such a fool of herself back at the picnic by throwing herself at him they'd still be friends. Life would still be peaceful.

With the salad made, she had twenty minutes to herself. Time to see if her résumé had hooked any interested employers. It was high time she got out of Cash's way—permanently.

She rushed to the computer. Her fingers flew over the keyboard. Though the thought of never seeing Cash again bothered her, she refused to dwell on it. Maybe by the end of the week she'd have an interview lined up—no, make that two or three.

Out of habit, she started to type the address for the Jiffy Cook website. She stopped herself just before hitting "enter." That was her past. Her future was waiting for her in her inbox.

With the correct address entered, her fingers

drummed on the oak desktop. At last the screen popped up. She had a number of new emails. She held her breath in anticipation as she opened the first one:

To: JiffyCook@myemail.com
From: admin@TheTurquoiseCantina.com
RE: Employment
Thank you so much for considering the Turquoise Cantina in your employment pursuit. However, at this time we don't have any openings. We wish you the best with your continued endeavors.

Disappointment slammed into Meghan. She hadn't realized until that moment how much she'd been counting on an eager reception to her inquiries.

She swallowed hard. There were still other responses. She opened each of them. One after the other. All were polite. But each held the same message: thanks, but no thanks.

Meghan's eyes stung as she stared at the monitor.

"Ready?"

The sound of Cash's voice jarred her from her thoughts. After a couple of rapid blinks she shut down the computer. She'd figure out what to do tomorrow. It'd always seemed to work for Scarlett O'Hara.

"I'll get your dinner," she muttered through clenched teeth. With her shoulders rigid, she strutted past him to retrieve a plate from the cabinet.

"Aren't you eating too?"

She could feel his curious stare drilling into the back of her head, but a girl could only take so much rejection without it getting to her. Cash hadn't just rejected her kiss, he'd then proceeded to treat her like she had the plague. She slammed the plate on the table.

"Would you talk to me?" Cash's voice rumbled with agitation. "Tell me what's bothering you."

With only seconds to go on the timer, Meghan turned off the oven and pulled the pizza out. She placed it on the stovetop and threw down the hot mitts.

Her patience stretched to the limit, she swung around to face him. "That's rich, coming from you. You've done nothing but give me the cold shoulder since I mistakenly tried to kiss you."

Cash crossed his arms, his face creased into a deep frown. "I thought I explained why starting anything between us would be a mistake. I should never have suggested the picnic. I'm sorry. Now, will you join me for dinner?"

"I'm not hungry."

He stepped closer. His voice lowered. "Listen, I know I've been a bear lately—"

"A bear with a thorn in his paw."

His lips pressed into a firm line. "I guess I deserve that. But if I promise to be on my best behavior will you eat dinner with me? After all, you have the baby to think of."

She shook her head. "I've got more than that on my mind."

"Such as?"

Her gaze met his. Genuine concern was reflected in his eyes. At last Cash was being his usual caring self. She breathed easier, knowing that the grouchy version of him was gone. Still, she wasn't so sure she was up for sharing her latest failure.

"Meg, I'm not going anywhere until you spit it out."

His unbending tone let her know that he was serious.

"Fine. If you must know I just got a slew of responses to my job search. Seems no one needs an out-of-work Jiffy Cook."

Cash stepped forward. His hands rose as if to embrace her. She glared at him. She didn't want his pity. Not now. She needed to hold it together. His arms lowered.

"Maybe I gave up on my television show too soon. I should ask—no, *beg*—for my job back."

"Don't do that. You already told me it didn't make you happy."

She clenched her fists. His calm, reasonable tone grated on her last nerve as panic twisted her stomach in knots. "But I don't have much savings. And with the baby coming I need a steady paycheck."

Cash pulled out a kitchen chair and helped her into it. He knelt down in front of her. "You tried—what? A half-dozen restaurants?" When she nodded, he continued, "There are dozens more you haven't contacted. Keep going. Keep trying. You'll find the right position in no time."

He was right. Her search had only just begun. Her stomach began to settle. "I know you're right. But with the baby on the way it's just so scary not to have a reliable job."

"Quit worrying. You and that little one will be just fine. My offer still stands. Any time you want some help—"

She shook her head. "I'm fine now. I can do this. But thank you."

He got to his feet. "Stay there. I'll get you a plate. And no protests. That little one you're carrying is hungry."

Cash amazed her with his ability to be so supportive. No one in her life had ever rallied behind her like he had. The others had barged in and told her what to do.

But not Cash. He was willing to step aside and let her find her own way. How would she ever repay him?

Cash chugged down his third mug of coffee and trudged off to the barn. Another yawn plagued him. After his talk with Meg the previous evening he'd been troubled by his conscience.

He'd spent a sleepless night, staring into the darkness, wrestling with what he should do: honor his word to Meg and let her find a job on her own? Or make a few phone calls on her behalf?

After witnessing the toll her unemployment was taking on her, he couldn't imagine that the ensuing stress was any good for the baby. And the knowledge that she was considering begging for her television job back tipped his decision.

He'd made a lot of contacts while working the rodeo circuit. After all, he was a world champion twice over. He'd had influential sponsors. He'd never asked for any special favors in the past so he had a few chips to cash in.

He was hesitant, though, to reconnect with that part of his life. He had always thought that when he'd decided to walk away after that last scandal selling horses to cowboys would be the extent of his involvement with the rodeo crew.

However, there was more here to consider than his own comfort. Meg and her baby deserved a good life, and if he could do anything to make that happen he had to at least try.

He grabbed for his phone. The echo of Meg's determined voice filled his mind. Surely she'd forgive him? After all, he was only offering her a helping hand.

He dialed the phone number scrawled on an old slip of paper. "Hey, Tex. It's Cash. I was hoping you could help me out with something…"

Meghan sat down at Cash's computer with her bottom lip clenched firmly between her teeth. A couple of days had elapsed since she'd received that handful of passes on her résumé, but after Cash's pep talk she'd contacted more potential employers. Now it was time to see if anyone was willing to give her a chance.

She sent up a short, hopeful prayer and opened her email. The first few were more of the same—"thanks, but no thanks" notes. The fourth email was from someone whose name and address she didn't recognize.

To: JiffyCook@myemail.com
From: Tex.Northridge1@emailRus.com

RE: Inquiry

Ms. Finnegan, it has come to my attention that you're looking for a position in the restaurant industry. I'm currently in the process of establishing the Golden Mesa Restaurant, a 5-star culinary delight in Albuquerque. If you were to forward me your résumé and a list of references, I'd like to consider you for our kitchen staff.

At last her luck was turning around. She couldn't quit grinning. She squealed with delight.

Cash ran into the room. "What's wrong? Is it the baby?"

"Nothing's wrong. Nothing at all."

She jumped to her feet. In a wave of happy adrenaline she rushed over, threw her arms around his neck and hugged him. At first he didn't move, but then his arms snaked around her blossoming waistline to give her a squeeze. It'd only take the turn of her head for them to be lip to lip.

He was so tempting.

So desirable.

So…

No. She couldn't set herself up to be rebuffed once again. If he wanted her, he'd have to make the first move.

She pulled back. Pretending not to be affected by their closeness, she explained to him about the email she had just received. "I don't know how the owner got my name, though."

Cash's throat bobbed. "Hey, you're a celebrity. I'm sure the word is out that your talent is available to the right restaurant."

"You really think people in the know are talking about me?"

"Of course I do. Did you email back?"

"No. I was so excited I forgot. But with it being Friday I probably won't hear back until Monday."

In that moment she realized her two weeks at the Tumbling Weed were almost over. She'd been hoping that by the time she had to face her family and friends she'd once again be gainfully employed.

"Don't worry," Cash said, as though reading her troubled thoughts. "We'll get through the weekend together. Maybe there will be some more murder mysteries on television for us to guess the culprit."

She smiled. Her chest was filled with a grateful warmth over the way he'd so smoothly made it possible for her to stay on a little longer without putting her in the difficult position of having to ask.

It'd all work out. She wasn't worried. She had a good feeling about this job—a real good feeling.

With a thump, she settled back into the desk chair. It was time to put her best foot forward. She began to type an eager response.

CHAPTER FIFTEEN

HE'D CHICKENED OUT.

After witnessing Meg's excitement over the job inquiry Cash hadn't been able to bring himself to snuff out her glow by confessing that he might have opened the door for her with Tex. Besides, all he'd done was make a few phone calls and throw out her name. It would be Meg's talent that landed her that job. And he had no doubt she'd get it.

In all honesty, it hadn't been easy to convince Tex to consider Meg. News of her canceled television show and the ensuing bad press hadn't died down yet. In an effort to counter the negativity Cash had mentioned in confidence Meg's upcoming cookbook deal, assuring Tex that the public would love it. In addition, Cash had thrown out the idea of having a large press presence and a sizeable crowd for the ribbon cutting. Tex had liked the thought of creating some media buzz about the grand opening.

Now Cash was in over his head. But he couldn't back out.

Tex had held up his end of the deal by taking Meg into consideration for executive chef. Now Cash had to come through with his part of the deal. And he wasn't looking forward to it.

But the thought of Meg and the baby with a secure future would make it tolerable. He'd do almost anything for them.

He'd done some research on the internet and now he had a plan of action. Only it'd take more manpower than he could muster single-handedly in such a short space of time. Remembering Meg's sister's phone number was still on his cell phone, he strode outside for privacy and placed a call. He could only hope her sister was as trusting of strangers as Meg.

A warm voice answered.

"Is this Ella? Meg's sister?" he asked, hoping he wasn't about to make a fool of himself.

"Possibly. And who would this be?"

She was cautious. Good for her.

"This is Cash Sullivan. I think your sister might have mentioned me."

"Is Meghan all right?" Ella asked in a rushed, anxious voice.

"Yes, she is. I didn't mean to alarm you. There's a problem, but it has nothing to do with her health."

"Did one of those reporters track her down? I told her eventually they'd find her. They're worse than bloodhounds."

His gaze moved to the empty country lane. "So far she's avoided them. The reason I'm calling is because I need your help if we're going to get your sister a new—a *better* job as the celebrity chef of a new five-star restaurant."

"I still can't believe they canceled her show." A note of anger rumbled through the phone. "You know, I saw Harold talking to some TV executives at the church. I'm certain he's somehow mixed up in this. I never did understand what Meghan saw in him."

That made two of them. But Cash didn't want to get started listing all Harold's faults or they might be there all evening. They had more pressing matters to discuss.

"Your sister is returning home soon, but it's going to be tough for her to face her friends and family with no husband and no job." He didn't elaborate on her need for this job because he wasn't going to spill the beans about the baby. Meg had a right to her privacy, as his grandmother had pointed out. "I have a plan, but we'll need to act fast."

"*We?* As in you and me?" Her tone sounded doubtful.

"Yes." His neck and shoulders tightened as he thought of the way this must sound to her.

"But I don't even know you."

"True. But what devious motive could I have by helping Meg get a job?"

A slight pause ensued. "Are you in love with her?"

What? Talk about a crazy idea—this ranked at the top of the list. It was a physical attraction between them—pure and simple.

"Of course not. Your sister has been a big help to me and my grandmother. All I want is a chance to pay her back."

"I'm listening."

"There's one condition, though. Would you be willing to keep this from Meg until we work out all the details?" He almost mentioned how the stress wouldn't be good for the baby. Instead he settled for, "After the wedding she was so upset she ended up physically sick. I don't want to get her worked up again, especially since she doesn't quite have the job yet."

"Aren't you rushing things, then?"

"I have faith in your sister's abilities."

"Are you sure there isn't something else going on between you two?"

Her suspicion made him uneasy. Memories of the steamy kiss they'd shared stirred his body. Did that constitute something going on? No.

He'd certainly made it to a lot more bases in the past without any strings attached. This was no different.

"I'm certain. She's a friend. Nothing more," he lied.

"If you say so."

She didn't sound as though she'd bought his line. Her warm voice was a lot like Meg's and, just like her sister, she wasn't easily swayed.

He brushed off Ella's suspicions. They had more important matters to address, and soon Meg would come looking for him for dinner. "The thing is, this will take more coordination and planning than I have time to do on my own. Will you help?"

"Depends on what you have in mind. Start talking."

Her interest in hearing him out eased his tension. With some help, his plan had a real chance. He prayed it would all work out the way he envisioned. Then Meg and the little one would have a stable, happy life—something *he* could never offer them.

Talk about a joyous homecoming.

Meg pulled up to the ranch house at Tumbling Weed after returning from her job interview on Tuesday morning with Tex Northridge. She smiled as she recalled how well the meeting had gone. She'd left him with a sample menu and he'd assured her that he'd be in contact "real soon."

She climbed out of the truck to find Cash standing on the porch as though he'd been there for a while, waiting for her. The thought filled her with warmth and her smile broadened.

"I'd ask how the interview went, but by the look on your face I'd say you have the job."

"Not quite. But I have a good feeling about it."

"I never doubted you could pull it off."

She climbed the steps and stopped next to him. "That's one thing I love about you." When surprise was reflected in Cash's gray eyes she realized her poor word choice hadn't gone unnoticed. Not wanting to make an even bigger deal of it, she continued, "You're always so encouraging and optimistic...about my life. I just wish you'd take some of your own advice. Forget your past and make a future for yourself."

He looked at her thoughtfully. "You still think that's possible after everything I've told you?"

"I honestly do. The trick is you have to believe it too."

Cash shuffled his feet. "We best get moving or we'll be late for lunch. And you know how Gram likes to eat on time."

"She's home?" Meghan grinned.

Cash nodded and led her back to the pickup.

She couldn't wait to see her dear friend. It felt like she'd been gone for a month or more. What was she going to do when she returned to Albuquerque? The thought of never seeing Martha—or Cash—deflated her good mood.

Lunch was filled with nonstop talk about Meghan's interview and Amy Santiago's babies. Cash remained unusually quiet and ducked back out the door before he even swallowed his last bite of sandwich.

After the dishes were washed and the kitchen put to rights Martha shooed her out. "Go and work on some new recipes for that cookbook."

"Are you sure? I could stay and help you unpack, or do laundry."

"Nonsense. You have more important things to do. And it's great you're putting my grandson's new kitchen to use."

"I can work on the recipes another time," Meghan insisted, preferring to stay here and talk.

"Go," Martha said, chasing her through the door. "I'll be over for dinner at six. Yell if you need any help."

My, how things were changing. Dinner at Cash's house and *she* was in charge of the meal. As Meghan strolled up the lane she realized those meals were numbered. She'd already stayed beyond what they'd originally agreed to. Once she heard back from Mr. Northridge, which was supposed to be by the end of this week, she'd be gone.

Sure, she could keep finding excuses to stay longer, and Cash was too much of a gentleman to boot her out. But it wasn't fair to him, and it was high time she stood firmly on her own two feet. If this job didn't pan out she'd find another.

She might have lost her television career, but her life wasn't over. In fact it was just beginning.

But somewhere along the way she'd started picturing Cash as part of that new beginning. Not a good thing to do with a man who'd shut himself off from love. If only she could get through to him…

Once she stepped into the kitchen she concentrated on creating fabulous new recipes. She whipped up sauces and marinades. She discarded the ones she'd classify as merely "good." She was looking for something with a "wow" factor. She knew Cash liked her cooking, but tonight she planned to knock his boots off.

All too soon the back door banged shut. Her gaze shifted to the wall clock above the sink. Half past five. When had it gotten so late? Martha would arrive soon and she wasn't ready.

Meghan dropped a hot mitt to the counter and

ran a hand over her hair. After slaving over the stove all afternoon she must look a sight, but it was too late to go spruce herself up.

Cash strode into the kitchen. "Something sure smells good."

"Thanks. Umm…I didn't have a chance to clean up. I was working on recipes for the cookbook."

"Does this mean we're going to dine on another of your soon-to-be famous recipes?"

"Are you offering to be my guinea pig again?"

His dimple showed when he smiled. "If it's as good as your other creations, count me in."

"You know I won't be around much longer to tempt your palate?"

The light in his eyes dimmed. She'd thought he'd be relieved to know he'd soon have the place back to himself. Was it possible he wasn't anxious for her to go?

Before she could figure out how to ask him such a delicate question he excused himself to go wash up for dinner.

He was so sweet and kind. It was a shame he had no intention of letting some lucky woman into his life. Next to her father, he was the most dependable man she'd ever known.

Meghan had finished setting the dining room table when Cash strolled back into the kitchen, looking fresh and dangerously sexy with his damp hair. His Western shirt was unbuttoned, giving her a glimpse of the light smattering of dark hair on his chest. Heat rushed to her cheeks and she glanced away, trying to focus on cleaning up the kitchen island.

He approached her and she inhaled a whiff of his spicy cologne. It was darn near intoxicating, and she nearly dropped the mixing bowl she'd intended to place in the sink. He reached out to take the bowl from her and their fingers connected.

The heat of his touch zinged up her arm and settled in her chest. She turned her head to him. His very kissable lips hovered only a few inches from hers. Would it be so wrong to take one more sizzling memory with her when she left?

She tried to tell herself this wasn't right—for either of them—but the pounding of her heart and the yearning in her core drove her beyond the bounds of caution.

The breath caught in her throat and the blood pounded in her veins. She was totally caught up in an overwhelming need to have him kiss her—here—now. For just this moment she wanted to forget their circumstances and lose herself in his arms.

His hungry gaze met and held hers. He wanted her too. She'd never experienced such desire. Her stomach quivered with excitement.

But she held herself back. She'd promised herself the next time *he'd* be the one to make the first move. She couldn't risk being shunned again—no matter how much she wanted him.

As though reading her thoughts, he lowered his head. Thankfully she didn't have to test her resolution. As light as a breeze, his lips brushed hers.

He pulled back ever so slightly. A frustrated groan clogged her throat. He couldn't stop yet. She needed more. Something hot and steamy to fill the long lonely nights ahead of her.

"Kiss me again," she murmured over the pounding of her heart. "Kiss me like there's no tomorrow."

His breath was rushed as it brushed her cheek. "You're sure?"

"Stop talking and press your lips to mine."

In the driver's seat, she reveled in the exhilaration of telling Cash what she desired. His eyes flared with passion before he obliged her by running his lips tentatively over hers. A moan swelled inside her and vibrated in her throat.

When he pulled back and sent her a questioning gaze, she said, "Again."

His mouth pressed to hers with urgency this time. As their kiss deepened excitement sparked and exploded inside her like a Roman candle. He sought out her tongue with his. He tasted fresh and minty. Her arms trailed around his neck and she sidled up against him. She wanted more of him—so much more.

In the background, she heard a bowl hit the countertop with a thud before his hands slid around her waist. His fingertips slipped beneath the hem of her top to stroke her tender flesh. She lifted her legs and wrapped them about his waist, never moving her mouth from his. His kisses were sweeter than honey and she was on a sugar high. She'd never get enough of him. *Ever.*

Just then it sounded like someone had cleared their throat, but Cash didn't miss a beat as he rained down sweet kisses on her. Obviously she'd been hearing things. She let herself once again be swept away in the moment.

"Excuse me?" The sound of Martha's voice startled Meghan, ending the kiss. "I hate to intrude, but I think something is burning."

Meghan lowered her feet to the floor as a blaze of heat flamed up her neck and set her cheeks on fire. She felt like a naughty teenager, having just been busted making out with the hottest guy in school.

"You need to do something with the stove." Martha pointed over Meghan's shoulder. "Dinner is going to be ruined."

"Dinner!" Meghan shrieked, coming out of her desire-induced trance.

She rushed to the stove, glad to have a reason not to face Martha. She had no excuse for losing her mind and begging Cash to kiss her. Between the steam from her sauce and the heat from her utter mortification she thought she was going to melt.

"Gram…we…um…didn't know it was so late," Cash stuttered.

"Obviously. Good thing I showed up before this place went up in smoke."

Martha's voice held a note of amusement, which only added to Meghan's discomfort.

Though the bottom layer of the Dijon sauce was burnt, she was able to ladle off enough for the three of them. Thankfully Martha didn't make a fuss about the scene she'd walked in on. In fact she seemed rather pleased with the idea—mistaken though it was—that they were a couple.

Someone needed to set Martha straight, but with Meghan's lips still tingling and her heart doing double-time she couldn't lie to the woman. There was no way she'd be able to convince anyone that the kiss had meant nothing to her. In fact it'd shaken her to her core.

Instead of saying goodbye, it had been more like hello.

* * *

Please ring.

Meghan lifted the phone Friday morning and checked for a dial tone. Satisfied it still worked since she'd checked it a half hour ago, she hung up. What was the problem? Why hadn't she heard about the job yet?

Maybe it was bad news and they were dragging their feet about making an uncomfortable call. Her stomach plummeted. Or it could be good news and they were notifying all of the other candidates first. Her spirits rose a little.

She sighed. Staring at the phone wouldn't make it ring. She needed to get busy if she was going to maintain her sanity. After all, there was a pile of dirty laundry with her name on it.

She'd just started up the stairs when the chime of the phone filled the air. Like a sprinter, she set off for the kitchen.

She paused, gathered herself, and blew out a deep breath.

"Hello?" She hoped her voice didn't sound as shaky as she felt.

"Good morning, Ms. Finnegan. This is Tex Northridge…"

In her frenzied mind his words merged into an excited blur. However, she caught the most important part—she'd got the job!

Her heart thump-thumped with excitement.

She grinned until her cheeks grew tired. She couldn't wait to tell Cash the news.

In the end, the position had come down to her and one other. It was her sample menu with its unique flair which she'd thought to include with her résumé that had tipped the balance in her favor. *She* would be the executive chef.

Still in a daze, she hung up the phone. At last she had what she'd wanted since she'd arrived at the Tumbling Weed—a new beginning for herself and the baby. She should be bubbling over with joy, but as her gaze moved around the room which had come to feel like home to her the smile slid from her face.

It was more than the house—it was Cash. Now that she had a job the time had come for her to leave…leave *him*. The thought tugged at her heart.

She shoved aside her tangle of feelings for the cowboy and forced her thoughts back to her new job. Her mouth gaped open when she realized in her excitement that she'd forgotten to ask how soon Mr. Northridge would need a full menu to approve. She immediately called back.

"I thought Cash would have told you," Mr. Northridge said. "We have the ribbon cutting coming up in a few weeks. We need to have everything in place by then."

Cash was involved in her getting this job?

Her heart rammed into her throat, choking her. *How? Why?* Questions bombarded her. She choked down her rising emotions. There had to be a mistake.

"Cash knows?"

"Well, sure. We go back a long way, to when he was a rodeo champ. So when he called me about you I was eager to help."

Stunned to the point of numbness, she asked, "This was his idea?"

"You're lucky to have a man who'll go out of his way for you. He's really outdone himself arranging press coverage. They're all anxious to find out what the Jiffy Cook is up to. It was a brilliant idea to reveal your upcoming cookbook deal at the restaurant opening."

She blinked repeatedly, holding back a wave of disappointment. Feeling as though someone had ripped out her heart, she hung up the phone.

Meghan sank down in a kitchen chair and rested her face in her hands. Cash was behind this whole job offer. He had gone behind her back and done exactly what she'd asked him not to do.

Her chest ached and her head throbbed. How could he have done this? She'd trusted him.

He was no better than her ex. He'd manipulated her into doing what he thought was right for her—or was it what worked for *him?*

CHAPTER SIXTEEN

THE CLOSER CASH got to the house, the faster he moved. He was a man on a mission and his plan was beginning to fall into place. The night before, when he'd taken Gram home, he'd explained about his involvement in getting Meg the interview. No arm twisting had been necessary to convince his grandmother to call her friends and invite everyone to attend the upcoming ribbon-cutting ceremony. The only part she'd balked at was keeping his involvement a secret from Meg, but upon revealing how Meg had refused his offer of help Gram had relented.

With it being almost lunchtime, he slipped off his boots and stepped into the kitchen, expecting to find Meg hard at work on a new recipe. The room was empty and the counters were spotless. He supposed it was possible she'd never returned from Gram's house after breakfast. He wouldn't know as he'd been busy in the tackroom, making phone calls and fighting with the internet to push ahead with advertising the big event.

"Meg?" No response. "Meg, are you here? It's time to head over to Gram's for lunch."

His mood had lifted ever since that kiss—the kiss Meg had insisted upon—the one that had spiraled so wonderfully out of control. If Gram hadn't intervened dinner wouldn't have been the only thing overheated.

The memory made his mouth go dry. The last thing he should do was stir up the embers, but he'd loved how he hadn't been the only one getting into the moment. Meg had been demanding and it had only heated his blood all the more.

"What are you smiling about?"

Meg's serious tone wiped the grin from his face.

"Nothing. Are you ready for lunch?"

"It can wait." She crossed her arms and her brows knit together in a frown. "We need to talk."

Oh, no. What had happened? His body grew tense.

"Why don't we eat first?" Somehow food seemed to calm people. "Gram will be waiting."

"I phoned Martha a while ago and explained that we'd be late." Meg didn't wait for him to say a word before she turned on her heels and headed for the family room.

His body tensed as he followed her rapid footsteps. What was bothering her? He couldn't think of anything he'd done wrong, but that didn't mean he hadn't missed something.

He followed her as far as the doorway, where he propped himself against the doorjamb. She paced in front of the stone fireplace, her forehead creased as though she were in deep thought.

His gut churned with dread. "Whatever it is, just spit it out."

She stopped and stared at him. "I got that executive chef position…but I'm sure that's no surprise to *you,* since Mr. Northridge said you went out of your way to make it happen."

Cash rubbed at the tightness in his chest. So much for keeping his involvement off the radar. And now that Meg knew she sure didn't look grateful. He'd guessed that one wrong.

"You aren't going to deny it?" When he shook his head, she continued, "How could you do it?"

Justification teetered on the tip of his tongue, but he knew it would be a waste of breath. He'd been busted. And it didn't matter that he'd had the best of intentions—he'd broken his word to her.

"I asked you to leave my employment issue alone, but you couldn't trust me to handle it. I was *so* wrong about you. You're just like my ex. Both of you think you know what's best for me. And you don't!"

Her comparison between him and Harold was like a sucker punch to the gut. "That's not true. I'm not like that jerk. It isn't like I dumped you at the altar. I only tried to help."

Meg pulled her shoulders back and jutted out her chin. "How? By helping me out the door?"

"That's not true."

"Why?" Her lips pursed together. "Are you saying you want me to stay?"

He couldn't give Meg the answer she wanted— the words inside his heart. It was impossible. He was crazy even to contemplate the idea.

The Sullivan men repeatedly hurt those around them. He thought of the physical and mental anguish he'd witnessed between his parents. And then how he'd come to the Tumbling Weed, where his grandfather had verbally abused him. The men in his family lacked the ability to be gentle and caring. But Meg had showed him that he wasn't like them. He was different. So what was holding him back?

Clarity struck with the force of a sharp blow to his chest. All this time he'd had it backward. It wasn't that he feared hurting her, but rather he feared that by letting her in she'd let him down—like most everyone else.

"Cash, say something." She wrung her hands. "Are you saying we have something beyond an employer/employee relationship?"

He wanted to say yes. He wanted to trust her and believe what she was saying. But once bitten, twice shy…

He swallowed hard. "Weren't you listening the other day in the meadow? I'm not good for you—for anyone."

"You're hiding away from life here on this ranch!" she shouted. "Any man who takes such loving care of his grandmother and takes in a total stranger is a good man."

Meg continued to cling to the idea that he could fit into her life like a dog clutching a bone. Cash's neck tensed. He had to get her to forget about this foolish notion.

"Meg, listen to me. I'm not the man for you. My past isn't dead and gone. It still haunts me. It will ruin your future."

"No, it won't. It's old news. The only one keeping it alive is you."

He wished she was right, but the reporter who'd visited the ranch proved his point. Now he had no choice but to reveal his latest embarrassing scandal.

Cash sucked in a deep breath and straightened his shoulders, feeling the heavy weight of his past pushing down on him. He slowly blew out a breath, all the while figuring out where to start.

"Remember how I told you I left the rodeo after I busted my shoulder?" When she nodded, he continued, "That wasn't the only reason I pulled out. My ex-girlfriend framed me for a robbery in Austin. Being a child armed robber sticks to a person worse than flypaper. The rodeo circuit is a small world and people have long memories. Even that reporter who showed up here knew all about my past. He accused me of moving from robbing liquor stores and rodeos to stealing the bride from her own wedding."

Sympathy was reflected in Meg's luminous green eyes as she stepped closer. Her tone softened but still held a note of conviction. "You've got to stand up and prove to everyone—most of all to yourself—that there's more to you than those nasty tabloid stories. You're a strong, hardworking cowboy who cares deeply about his family."

Cash had never thought anyone would fight for him—certainly no one as special as Meg. In the time they'd spent together she'd snuck past his defenses and niggled her way into his heart, filling it up—making him whole.

But she didn't belong here at the Tumbling Weed. Her future was in the spotlight. Soon she'd realize that and then she'd be miserable here.

The thought of what he had to do next turned his stomach. He met Meg's determined gaze head-on. She refused to back down.

You can do this. It's the best thing for her.

"I need you to listen to me," he said. "You've read too much into what we've shared."

She shook her head. "I *know* you felt that strong connection too."

He had, but that was beside the point. Right now it was about getting her to see sense.

"It was a physical thing," he forced out. "Nothing more."

He stood rigid, resisting the urge to turn away and miss the pain that was about to filter through her emerald eyes. It would serve as his punishment for letting himself get too close to someone—a lesson he would never forget.

You can do this. You're almost there.

Soon Meg would be set free to have the wonderful life she deserved.

He swallowed. "I knew things were getting out of control between us. That's why I contacted Tex. It's…it's time you got on with your life—"

"Stop." She held out a shaky hand. "I don't want to hear any more."

Her eyes shimmered with unshed tears. She pressed a hand to her mouth and fled the room.

He felt lower than pond scum. What had he done?

He followed, but she'd already made it to the second floor. The resounding bang of her bedroom door shattered the eerie silence.

"I'm so sorry. I only wanted what was best for you and the baby."

The too-late words floated up the empty staircase and dissipated. He felt more alone in that moment than he had ever felt in his life.

Meghan sat by the bedroom window as tears fell one after the other. Stupid hormones had her crying over every little thing. It wasn't like Cash had told her anything she didn't already know. Of *course* there was nothing between them.

Memories of the moments she'd spent in his arms flooded her mind. The kisses they'd shared—had they all been a fleeting fancy for him? How could that be?

They'd been so much more for her. Why, oh, why had she read so much into his soft touches and passionate embraces?

Every time she replayed how he'd admitted he'd found the job for her so she'd leave, the aching hole in her chest widened. She blamed her out-of-control emotions on her pregnancy. In the future she'd work harder at keeping them under wraps.

When she saw Cash jump into his pickup to head over to Martha's for lunch she knew her time at the Tumbling Weed was up. She needed to head home and face the music—or, in her case, face her mother and any lingering reporters.

CHAPTER SEVENTEEN

ONE LONELY, MISERABLE week stretched into two…then three.

All alone, Cash stood in his kitchen, holding a mug full of coffee. His thoughts strolled back to the day Meg had left him, leaving only a brief note thanking him for his hospitality. Instead of asking him for a ride into town she'd called upon his ranch foreman, Hal, whom she'd befriended during her stay. Cash hated how she'd slipped away without so much as a "good to know you," but he couldn't blame her after his not-so-gentle letdown.

Without her around, the house was so quiet it was deafening. There was nowhere to go, and nothing he did let him escape his thoughts. He couldn't hide behind the excuse that by turning her away he'd done the right thing. The glaring truth was he'd let her go because he was afraid of taking a chance on love.

He gazed out the kitchen window as the late

evening sun glowed liked a fireball, painting the distant horizon with splashes of pink and purple. Still he frowned.

A sip of the now-cold brew caused him to grimace and dump the remainder down the drain. Food no longer appealed to him. It was just one more reminder of Meg. Not even Gram's down-home cooking stirred his appetite. Everything tasted like sawdust.

Everywhere he looked he saw Meg's image. Next to the stove, serving up eggs and bacon. In the laundry room, folding his clothes. In the family room, watching television. Even the stables didn't provide him with an escape. Her memory lurked in every inch of the Tumbling Weed.

While doing some overdue soul-searching he'd realized he had accomplished something his father never had—he owned his own home. And he couldn't imagine ever demeaning anyone the way his grandfather had done.

Could Meg be right?

Had he avoided the Sullivan curse?

Cash sighed. What good did the knowledge do him now? He'd already turned Meg away, and each day he regretted that decision even more.

He'd tried to move on with his life, but it was so hard when he was working night and day to make her new career a huge splash in all the news outlets. It was his parting gift to her and the sweet baby she was carrying. Sadness engulfed him as he thought of all he would miss.

The telephone buzzed, drawing him from his list of regrets. He grabbed the phone, but before he could utter a greeting he heard, "Cash, what exactly did you do to my sister?"

The female voice was familiar, but it definitely didn't belong to Meg. "Ella? Is that you?"

"Of course it's me. How many women do you have calling you about their sister?"

The implication of her initial accusation sank in. "What's wrong with Meg? Is it the—?"

He stopped himself before blurting out about the baby. He recalled how Meg had planned to keep the pregnancy to herself for a while. The last thing he wanted to do was further complicate her life.

"The baby is fine," Ella said, as though reading his thoughts. "She had a doctor's appointment earlier this week and she got a clean bill of health."

"What's wrong with Meg?"

"She doesn't laugh," Ella said in an accusatory tone. "She doesn't smile. She wasn't this way until she stayed at your ranch. What happened? Did you break her heart?"

Was it possible Meg missed him as much as he missed her? Was there still hope for them?

Nonsense. She'd hate him by now.

"Meg will be fine." It was what he'd told himself every day since she'd left the Tumbling Weed. "She's probably just nervous about the new job. Wait until she sees everything that's planned for the ribbon-cutting ceremony."

"That's another thing. Do you know how hard it's been to keep her away from the internet? I think we should let her in on all of the details."

"Is everything in place?"

"Yes."

He supposed there was no longer a reason to keep Meg in the dark. "Go ahead and tell her how her publisher has agreed to go public at the ceremony with news of her three-book deal. It'll cheer her up."

"I hope so. Nothing else has." Ella sighed. "I could show her the outpourings of caring viewers on the new blog we set up for the Jiffy Cook cookbook series. The response has been huge. I can't believe we pulled this off."

"You did most of it," he said, not wanting to share the spotlight. He preferred to remain the man behind the curtain.

"You know that's not true. You've worked round the clock, drumming up support and lining up press coverage. It's amazing what you've been able to accomplish in such a short amount of time. When Meghan finds out how you went above and beyond for her she'll be indebted to you."

"No."

"What do you mean, *no?*"

"I don't want her to know I'm still involved. She'll think I'm trying to control her life."

"No, she won't. She'll be grateful."

"Trust me. I know your sister, and the less said about my involvement the better."

"You're acting just as strange as Meghan. I'm thinking there was a lot more cooking at your ranch than those recipes for the cookbook."

"The past is the past. Leave it be. After tomorrow afternoon Meg won't have time to think about her stay at the Tumbling Weed. She'll have a classy kitchen to run and a baby to plan for."

"You're going to be at the ceremony, aren't you?"

He shouldn't go. For his sake as well as Meg's. But the thought of seeing her just one more time—even from a distance—was too tempting to pass up.

"I promised my grandmother I'd drive her."

Meghan rushed into the bedroom of her Albuquerque apartment, clutching the now signed custody papers. She'd just come from a meeting with Harold. He hadn't changed his mind about the baby—he didn't want to be involved in any part of its life, and had willingly signed away his rights.

She couldn't believe she'd come so close to marrying a man so different from herself. And then there was Cash, who'd missed out on a chance to be a father—something he wanted. She was certain he'd make a fine parent if he would give himself the chance.

"About time you got here," Ella said, entering the bedroom. "You'll have to hurry or you'll be late for the ceremony."

Meghan stuffed her copy of the custody papers in her purse before going to touch up her barely there make-up. Her hand trembled, smearing brown eyeliner.

With the custody issue settled she should be focused on her career, but all she could think about was Cash. Every time her phone rang she hoped it would be him. But not once in the past few weeks had he attempted to contact her.

Was it possible he'd dismissed everything they'd shared so easily? The thought whipped up a torrent of frustration. Did he *have* to be so stoic and resolute about his lonely life?

Her wounded pride was willing to wallow in his rejection, but her heart wasn't ready to lie down and accept defeat. His spine-tingling kisses had contained more than raw hunger. They'd been gentle and loving. And she recalled how he'd opened up to her about his past. He'd let her in and revealed his vulnerable side. He wouldn't have done that with just anyone. He cared about her, and somehow she had to get him to admit it.

"I'm so nervous I can't hold my hand steady enough to put on my make-up." Meghan tossed the eyeliner pencil on the counter. "At this rate I'm going to look like a clown."

Ella walked over, handed her a tissue, and propelled her toward the bathroom. "Wash off your face and we'll start over. We don't want the Golden Mesa's executive chef looking anything but phenomenal in front of the press."

"I can't believe you pulled all this together. I couldn't have asked for a better sister."

"Hey, what about me?" chimed in her little sis Katie.

Meghan peeked her head around the doorway. "Correction. I couldn't have asked for *two* better sisters. You guys rock."

She added a few drops of water to the tissue and some facial cleanser. Even though she'd made a mess of her life her sisters were right there, rallying behind her. Thank goodness. At last her siblings had set aside their problems and banded together. Why in the world had she thought she had to go through all this alone? She should count her blessings, but a part of her wished Cash could be there for her too.

Her mother, on the other hand, had been mortified when she'd learned the reason for Meghan's disappearing act. Meghan scrubbed at the messed-up make-up with more force than necessary. Her mother hadn't been quiet about her disapproval over the way Meghan had handled the situation with the wedding. In fact she'd flat out refused to attend today's ribbon cutting.

What surprised Meghan the most was her ability to accept her mother's decision to stay away. She might love her mother, but it didn't mean they were good for each other. They'd always had a strained relationship. There was no reason to think it would change now...or ever.

"If you scrub your face much longer there won't be anything left," Ella called out. "And we've got to go soon."

Meghan glanced in the mirror at her blotchy complexion, noticing the dark shadows under her eyes. Her sister had her work cut out for her if she was going to make her look more human again instead of like something the cat dragged in.

"What's up with you? You sure don't look thrilled about finding such a great job," Katie said.

Ella elbowed their younger sister, frowning at her to be quiet.

Meghan pulled her shoulders back and tried not to frown. "Sorry, guys. I just have a lot on my mind."

"I thought landing the top position at a five-star restaurant would be a dream come true." Katie flounced down on the bed next to her and crossed her legs. "I'd love it if someone would give *me* a kitchen to run. Can you imagine all of the chocolate desserts I could create?"

Meghan found herself smiling at her little sister's different take on life. "We could swap places today."

Both sisters froze. Their smiles faded and they turned startled glances in her direction.

"Would you guys quit staring at me like my face has broken out in an ugly rash?" Meghan pressed her fingers to her cheeks, relieved to find no hot bumps.

Ella turned to grab some foundation from the dresser. "It's just that we've never heard you talk like this before. Your career has always been so important to you."

"Yeah," Katie chimed in. "You don't seem the least bit excited about today."

Meghan mentally admonished herself. Her sisters had chipped in with her boss to make this grand opening a huge event, and she was being nothing but a downer. "I think it must be these hormones. They have me moody most of the time."

Ella dabbed make-up on her cheeks. "I'd be willing to bet it isn't hormones. In fact I'd wager my bakery that your problem has something to do with a cowboy named Cash Sullivan."

"I agree," Katie piped up as she started to brush Meghan's hair.

The breath stilled in her lungs. How had they found out? She'd made sure to say very little about him since she'd come home. "What do you two know about him?"

Ella flashed her a guilty look. "I promised not to tell you, but…"

CHAPTER EIGHTEEN

"STEP ON IT, Cash," Gram insisted.

He chanced a startled glance at his grandmother. "Aren't you the one who usually tells me to slow down?"

"This is different. It's an emergency."

Since when had a ribbon-cutting ceremony qualified as an emergency? But he wasn't about to argue. He pressed harder on the accelerator. It felt like an eternity had passed since Meg had left. Enough time for him to realize that she'd not only invaded every part of his life but most especially his heart.

He'd finally had to accept that life was a series of choices. And now he had to face the most important choice of his life. Stay secluded on the Tumbling Weed and miss out on the good things life has to offer, or go after the woman he'd come to love—the woman who'd given him the desire and courage to admit he wanted to be a family man.

He chose to have Meghan in his life.

One question still remained: would she still want him?

His chest tightened with nervous tension as he braked for yet another red light. They were only seconds away from the Golden Mesa Restaurant.

Until now he'd been so anxious to set things straight with Meg that he hadn't taken time to contemplate the scene he'd have to face. The parking lot would be swarming with press. He'd made sure of it.

With each passing second the churning in his gut grew more intense. When the light changed, he tramped on the gas pedal. He'd wanted Meg to get as much coverage as possible to undo the damage her canceled television show and runaway bride episode had done to her reputation. While he'd been talking to the reporters over the phone about the ceremony he'd been able to cover up his own identity. But once he stepped anywhere near Meg the camera flashes would start, followed by probing questions.

His hands grew moist against the steering wheel. But he had to do this—there was no backing out now. Meg had finally opened his eyes and he accepted that he could never have anything worthwhile unless he was willing to accept the inherent risks.

He didn't want to end up a lousy husband,

like his father and grandfather. All he could do was promise Meg to do his best not to fall into bad habits. With her at his side, he believed he could be a husband and father worthy of his family's love.

Parked cars lined both sides of the street. Couples, families, young and old all filed down the sidewalk headed toward the restaurant. The turnout was phenomenal.

"There!" Gram shouted. "Someone's pulling out. Grab that parking spot."

"But it's a hike to the restaurant. I'll drop you off and then park."

Gram smacked his arm. "I'm not a helpless old lady. And we don't have time for you to play the thoughtful gentleman. You have to find Meghan and set things straight."

His grandmother was right. He was running out of time to find Meg before she took the stage. He glanced at his watch. Seven minutes until the ceremony began. The twisted knot inside him ratcheted tighter, squeezing the air from his lungs.

They parked and Cash rushed to help his grandmother out of the vehicle. Gram still got around quite well for her age, but as they started down the walk her modest pace held him back. He checked the time again. It would all work out. He forced a deep breath into his lungs.

"What are you doing?" Gram grumbled.

"Walking with you. What else would I be doing?"

"How about hurrying to the woman you love? Unless you've changed your mind about marrying her?"

He shook his head. He had doubts about being here, around all this press, but he didn't have any doubts about proposing.

"Then go," Gram said. "Don't let her get away. Tell her how you feel."

"Are you sure you'll be all right walking on your own?" he asked, not wanting to leave her alone in this crowd.

"I promise I won't get lost."

"Thanks, Gram." He kissed her cheek.

He sprinted up the walk, weaving his way through the throng of people. He couldn't miss this chance to prove to Meg that he'd changed— that at last he was ready to take a chance. A chance on *them*.

The number of supporters in the Golden Mesa parking lot was impressive. Ella had been right about advertising free giveaways—who didn't like something for nothing? They were also providing finger food, balloons and a Mariachi band. It was a very festive gathering, with lots of smiles.

The attendance surpassed Cash's wildest estimations. In fact there were so many people he had trouble threading his way to the stage. Tex Northridge stood in the spotlight, holding the microphone as he extolled the virtues of the newly opening Golden Mesa. Cash didn't have time to stop and listen.

He moved faster, bumping into people in his haste, yelling an apology over his shoulder. His gaze scanned left and right. Where in the world *was* she?

"Cash?" a female voice called out.

He stopped and turned, finding a woman waving her arms over her head. She looked familiar, but he couldn't put a name to the face. He considered ignoring her, but she might know Meg's whereabouts. He sidled over to the stranger and gave her a puzzled look. When she smiled, she bore a striking resemblance to Meg.

"Are you Ella?"

She eyed him and then smiled. "Good guess."

"Do you know where Meg is?"

She eyed him again. "What do you want with her?"

He deserved her suspicion. He just didn't have time to answer all her impending questions. "Let's just say I came to my senses. Now, where's your sister?"

"Well, it's about time you admitted it. She's over there."

He followed the line of her finger and spotted

Meg just as she stepped onto the stage. The only way to convince her that he was willing to do whatever was necessary to make this relationship work was to step up on that stage with her. He had to show her that he was stronger than those tabloid stories—that at last he was willing to step forward and take chances.

The closer he got to the stage, the more his gut churned. His gaze swept over the sea of unfamiliar faces and the army of cameras. His chest tightened to the point where he could barely suck in a breath. Maybe he should wait here in the shadows until Meg had given her speech.

Yet if he fell back into his old routine and shied away from the public…if he didn't make the choice to step outside of his comfort zone… how would he prove that he'd changed? If he couldn't make the right choice now, what made him think he'd have the courage, the strength, to do right by Meg and her baby?

Meghan stood in front of the microphone. "Thank you all for coming here today." She swallowed, easing the tickle in the back of her throat. "I'm so honored to have been offered the awesome position to head up the kitchen at the Golden Mesa, as well as to be offered a cookbook deal. Dreams really do come true!"

A round of applause filled the air.

Meghan's insides quivered with nerves. As she stood there she was more certain than ever of what she had to do. She was about to tell everyone how much she appreciated their support, but she couldn't accept the Golden Mesa position.

When Ella had spilled the beans about Cash being the mastermind behind this amazing ceremony it had confirmed that he still had feelings for her.

In the past couple of months she'd learned that life didn't always have to follow a plan—sometimes the best things in life came when you least expected them. Her mind filled with Cash's image. She knew exactly what she wanted—Cash. But first he'd have to admit he loved her. And the only way to find out was to go back to the one place she'd been happiest.

Frustration knotted up her stomach when she realized that for all of her best intentions—her attempts to put herself out there and chase after her dreams—she'd failed to do the most important thing of all.

She'd never spoken the actual words "I love you" to Cash.

Tex Northridge took control of the microphone. "Wait until you see the carefully planned menu we have to tempt your tastebuds!"

Meghan caught sight of Cash stepping onto the stage. What was he doing here?

"Ladies and gentlemen," continued Mr. Northridge, "in order to share this culinary experience with many of you, we have a number of gift cards to give away to some lucky winners."

Another round of applause and whistles filled the air, but all Meghan heard was the pounding of her heart. Her gaze remained glued to the rugged cowboy stepping into the spotlight. The fact he was willing to push past his fear of standing in front of a swarm of reporters to get to her made her love him all the more.

She wanted to run to him and shield him from the cameras, but her rubbery legs refused to move. A hush fell over the crowd. Even Mr. Northridge paused as Cash crossed the stage. He dropped to his knee and took her left hand in his. Camera flashes flared in the background, lighting up the sky like the Fourth of July.

"What are you doing?" she whispered.

He smiled up at her, causing her stomach to flutter and rob her of air. "I came here to stake my claim on the woman I love."

The fluttering in her chest increased and she grew giddy. Had she heard him correctly? She stared into his unwavering gaze. He was perfectly serious. "But you didn't have to come here. In front of everyone."

"Yes, I did. You taught me that I can't run or hide from my past. I no longer need to lurk in the shadows, always worrying about someone digging up ancient history."

"Oh, Cash." She swiped at her moist cheeks. "You're a great man, inside and out. Anyone who can't see that is blind."

His grip on her hand tightened. "Miss Meghan Finnegan, I love you."

This was her chance to put herself out there in front of everyone and reach for her dream—her happiness. "I love you too."

His confident gaze held hers. "Would you agree to be my bride?"

Her free hand pressed on her abdomen. The public didn't know she was in the family way, and she didn't want to announce it here, but she hoped Cash would know what she meant.

"Are you sure? I come with a lot of baggage."

"I wouldn't have you any other way. I love you and all of your baggage."

She pulled on his hand until he got to his feet, and then she held up her index finger for him to wait. She turned back to Tex Northridge and retrieved the microphone.

"Wow! I can't believe this day. I think I must be—no, I *know* I am the luckiest woman in the world. Thank you, everyone, for sharing this special moment with me." Tears of joy slipped down her cheeks.

Her new boss's brow arched. "Are you sure you want to pin your future on this cowboy?"

She couldn't think of anything she wanted more. She grinned. "I'm absolutely positive."

"Then let me be the first to congratulate you both." Mr. Northridge's tanned face lifted into a smile as he leaned toward Meghan. Loudly he said teasingly, "I hope Cash knows what a wonderful woman he's getting."

Cash stepped up and placed an arm around her waist. "I'm the luckiest man in the world."

Her unwavering gaze held his.

The crowd broke out into applause, shouting, "Kiss her!"

Cash swept her into his arms. "I've wasted enough time. What would you say to a brief engagement?"

He pulled her close for a deep, soul-searing kiss that gave way to a round of hootin' and hollerin' from the onlookers.

"I'd say when do we leave on the honeymoon?"

* * * * *

COMING NEXT MONTH from Harlequin® Romance
AVAILABLE AUGUST 6, 2013

#4387 THE COWBOY SHE COULDN'T FORGET
Slater Sisters of Montana
Patricia Thayer
Ana Slater knows she can't look after her ranch alone. Her only hope is the cowboy she has found it impossible to forget—Vance Rivers.

#4388 A MARRIAGE MADE IN ITALY
Rebecca Winters
Leon Malatesta is fiercely protective of his baby daughter. But does Belle Peterson's arrival bring the possibility of a new future for all of them?

#4389 MIRACLE IN BELLAROO CREEK
Bellaroo Creek
Barbara Hannay
Ed Cavanaugh always knew Milla Brady deserved true love. So when he arrives in Bellaroo Creek, he resolves to tell her how he truly feels....

#4390 THE COURAGE TO SAY YES
Barbara Wallace
Abby Gray needs a fresh start to finally put the past behind her. Can Hunter Smith convince her that happy-ever-afters do happen in real life?

You can find more information on upcoming Harlequin® titles, free excerpts and more at www.Harlequin.com.

HRLPCNM0713

SPECIAL EXCERPT FROM

 HARLEQUIN®

Romance

*Don your Stetson and your cowboy boots as
Patricia Thayer brings you first loves, second
chances and happy-ever-afters in the*
SLATER SISTERS OF MONTANA *series.*

ANA NEVER WAS one to take risks. She was the oldest, the sensible daughter. She always tried to do the right thing. So why was she walking across the compound to Vance's house just before dawn? She was afraid to even answer that question. She was shaking as she walked up the steps, then before she could chicken out, she knocked on the door. She stood there a few minutes and almost felt relieved when there wasn't an answer. Just as she started to leave, the door opened and Vance stood there wearing only a pair of jeans and a towel draped around his neck.

Oh, God. She loved looking at this man. She met his eyes and tried desperately to speak, but nothing came out of her mouth.

He reached for her, pulled her into the house and closed the door, pushing her back against it. A soft light came from over the stove in the kitchen, letting her see the look of desire in his eyes.

"What are you doing here?"

"I didn't like how we left things last night."

"So you thought coming here just before dawn was a wise thing to do?"

"I couldn't sleep."

"Join the club, lady. You've kept invading my dreams ever since you've come back home."

His honesty shocked her. "Really?"

In answer, he lowered his head and covered her mouth with his. With a soft moan, she gripped his bare arms, feeling his strength. Yet he held her with tenderness as he placed teasing kisses against her lips.

"We could bring my dreams to life if you like," he told her before he gave her another sample. He captured her mouth in a deep kiss, causing her knees to give out.

He wrapped his arms around her, pulling her close. "I got you," he whispered.

She laid her head against his chest, feeling his rapid heartbeat. "I've always wanted you, Vance," she breathed.

THE COWBOY SHE COULDN'T FORGET
by Patricia Thayer is available August 2013 only from Harlequin® Romance.